1 MONTH OF
FREE
READING

at

www.ForgottenBooks.com

By purchasing this book you are eligible for one month membership to ForgottenBooks.com, giving you unlimited access to our entire collection of over 1,000,000 titles via our web site and mobile apps.

To claim your free month visit:

www.forgottenbooks.com/free603440

ISBN 978-0-484-42934-4
PIBN 10603440

LOVE'S PROGRESS.

BY THE AUTHOR OF

"THE RECOLLECTIONS OF A NEW-ENGLAND HOUSE-
KEEPER," "THE SOUTHERN MATRON," ETC.

Gilman, Caroline (Howard)

> "I know not
> How I shall draw her pictnre; the young heart
> Has such restlessness of change, and each
> Of its wild moods so lovely!
> *   *   *   *
> Light to thy path, young creature!"
>   N. P. WILLIS.

NEW-YORK:

HARPER & BROTHERS, 82 CLIFF-STREET.

———

1840.

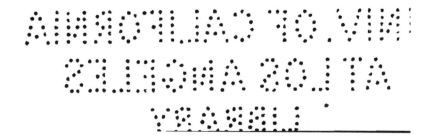

CONTENTS.

CHAPTER I.

The Baptism . . . . Page 9

CHAPTER II.

A tranquil Morning.—Ruth Raymond a Schoolgirl.—Ruth's Confession.—Skipping-rope.—Ruth's Present.—Childhood among Flowers.—Ruth's Love appears in a Name.—Effects of Ridicule.—
Willie White's Gallantry.—His Philosophy.—Ruth's first Dream
dissolved 12

CHAPTER III.

The Naturalist.—Ruth's Prejudice.—The Cure.—Her Sense of Justice disturbed.—The Butterfly Race.—Ruth's Danger.—Change of
Feeling.—Doubts 17

CHAPTER IV.

Dancing.—Monsieur Lagrande.—Right Appreciation of Motives.—
Ruth's Dancing.—Her second Preference.—An awkward Predicament.—A Change 23

CHAPTER V.

Ruth's Singing.—A Mother's Mistake.—A Question about Birds.—
Ruth falls into Extremes.—A Glimpse at the Future.—Angel
Choirs 27

CHAPTER VI.

Young Things.—Ruth too old for Dolls.—The Doll Family.—A Letter.—Ruth's Favourite.—A solemn Conclusion . . . 30

CHAPTER VII.

The Sleep of Childhood.—Its Terrors.—A Story from Dr. Gesner.—
Ruth's Distress.—Its Cure 36

CHAPTER VIII.

Ruth not a Genius.—The promised Prize at School.—Dangers of the
System.—Effect on Ruth.—Ruth's Triumph.—The Exhibition.—
Abby Mansfield.—Ruth's Mortification and Self-Conquest.—The
Prize awarded .   .   .   . Page 41

CHAPTER IX.

Friendship's first Grief.—The new Friend.—Patronage and Love.—
First reading of Shakspeare.—The Kitten Perdita's Danger.—Its
Rescue 45

CHAPTER X.

Ruth's Bedroom.—Her Library.—Love Tokens.—Music.—Romances.—Ruth writes Poetry 52

CHAPTER XI.

The Age of Presumption.—Despondency.—Religious Love . 57

CHAPTER XII.

Ruth Sixteen.—Her Apartment.—Seals.—Ruth Romantic.—Her
Mortification.—Development of Mind.—Invitation to a Ball . 60

CHAPTER XIII.

A Funeral Bell.—The Village Burial.—Ruth and a Stranger . 64

CHAPTER XIV.

Ruth's Sabbath and Church 68

CHAPTER XV.

Dresses of Heroines in Novels.—Heroines of Poetry.—Ruth and her
Mantuamaker.—Progress of Mind.—Ruth at the Ball.—New Acquaintance.—An Accident 74

CHAPTER XVI.

The Morning Slumberer.—The Cape Ann Housemaid.—The Morn-
ing-call.—Sunday-school Project.—The Farmer and his Wife.—
The Intemperate.—The Poor and Suffering 84

CHAPTER XVII.

Ruth's Reflections at Home.—More Experiences of Human Nature.
—The Sunday-school Opens.—Ruth Compensated .   . 94

CHAPTER XVIII.

The Sleigh-ride.—An Overturn.—Excitement.—William a Rich Man.—An Offer of Marriage . . . . . . Page 100

CHAPTER XIX.

Ruth's Grotto.—A Sister's Love.—New Sensations . . . 104

CHAPTER XX.

Delicate Positions. — Ruth's Character unfolds. — Glimpses into Hearts 108

CHAPTER XXI.

Ruth's Singing.—A Letter.—The case of Leeds and Whittesby.— Ruth Weeps.—A Denouément expected 113

CHAPTER XXII.

The Interview.—A Thunder-storm.—Ruth a Creature to be Loved 118

CHAPTER XXIII.

A Cloud on Ruth's Happiness.—A Promise.—Death . . . 123

CHAPTER XXIV.

Ruth and her Father.—The Burial 129

CHAPTER XXV.

The Raymond Fête 134

CHAPTER XXVI.

Clarendon Unhappy.—Ruth and her Pastor.—A Renewal of Vows 141

CHAPTER XXVII.

The Night succeeding the Ball 147

CHAPTER XXVIII.

The Departure 152

CHAPTER XXIX.

Clarendon's Visit to the Village.—A Letter.—An Interview . 158

CHAPTER XXX.

Trenton Falls 165

LOVE'S PROGRESS.

CHAPTER I.

THE BAPTISM.

ONE bleak wintry morning, the inhabitants of a village on the banks of the Hudson were gathering at their church, which stood on the sloping side of a hill. The mountain summits around were crowned with snow, icicles hung glittering from the trees, and the river lay bound in fetters ; but this did not prevent the "assembling themselves together" of the people. Sleigh-bells jingled merrily up the slippery ascent, boys were seen stamping the recent snow from their feet as they entered the porch, while the careful students of comfort deposited footstoves in their pews, with the quick salutation of a wintry day to their neighbours, as they pulled to the doors with an extra effort at closeness.

The venerable preacher, who, careless of the frost of the season, entered with the rest, was one of the last of the good old race, now gathered to their reward, who had wrestled body and soul for his country's freedom. His first prayer was concluded, and, descending from the pulpit, his gray locks falling gently forward, with a tremulous voice he said,

" Let the child be presented for baptism."

There was silence in the audience, except where the

younger members, climbing eagerly on their seats on tiptoe, broke the hush with their unsteady movements, and in the pew of the candidate for baptism. The warm garments that maternal care had wrapped around the sleeping babe were laid aside; and the mother, taking the child in her arms, whose long white robe almost swept the floor, followed with a light tread the more manly footsteps of her husband through the aisle, and stood with him before the pastor. Removing his spectacles, and passing his handkerchief over his still serene forehead, he bent forward and thus addressed them:

"It is fitting that we should dedicate to God the gifts which we receive from him. It is proper that we should invoke the blessing of heaven on the little beings who are just commencing the uncertain career of life. It is right that we should obey an express command of our Master and Saviour Jesus Christ. Let us not perform this solemn rite with rashness or indifference. Let us be reminded of our own baptismal vows and Christian obligations. Let us give this child to God with a fixed determination to abide by his gracious will respecting it, and with earnest and hearty prayers for its usefulness and happiness. Frail and feeble, yet precious little being! I welcome thee into the world, and into the external, visible church of Christ. I ask of God to bless thee. I ask of thy parents to watch over thy dawning character, to cherish every good and to crush every bad tendency which thy unfolding heart may exhibit. I ask them to train thee up for virtue, for happiness, and religion. Long mayst thou live a blessing to society and to the church. Mayst thou extract every pang from thy parents' bosoms, but never mayst thou plant one there; and when at length thou art called away from this checkered state, mayst thou be received into the bosom of thy Father and thy God."

The babe still slept, its mottled hands folded on a breast more tranquil than a waveless sea. Softly the mother laid it in its father's arms, gently the minister touched its soft forehead with the emblematic element, and pronounced in a clear voice the name of *Ruth.*

A tender and sweet solemnity dwelt on every parent's heart as the young mother, after the close of the ceremony, retraced her steps through the aisle, while the children of the church softly struggled to gain a glance of the little being who was now dedicated to God— was one of them.

There were four Ruths in the family of Mr. Raymond, the father of the babe ; one a great grandmother, hanging in the hall, faded and soiled, with a dreary-looking gash on the nose from the rudeness of soldiery in the revolutionary war ; near her was her daughter, with a starched white kerchief lying in folds over a rich damask dress, and the hair drawn tightly back from a fine open forehead ; then there was the picture of the present Mrs. Raymond in the parlour, a delicate-looking girl smelling a rosebud ; and lastly Ruth, the babe, a living picture, fresh from the masterly hand of creation, the heroine of my tale.

There is something almost melancholy in a prospective glance at the life of an infant. What an ocean is to heave from that little rill which is now gliding merrily among the green turf of existence !

CHAPTER II.

A tranquil Morning.—Ruth Raymond a Schoolgirl.—Ruth's Confession.—Skipping-rope.—Ruth's Present.—Childhood among Flowers.—Ruth's Love appears in a Name.—Effects of Ridicule.—
Willie White's Gallantry.—His Philosophy.—Ruth's first Dream
dissolved.

VERY delicious is the hush of a house after the departure of active children to their morning-school.
The darkened apartments, and the relaxed steps of
hitherto bustling servants as they deposite brooms and
brushes in retired closets for the ensuing twenty-four
hours, announce the housewife's and mother's holyday.
With her children's parting kiss fresh upon her lips,
and the echo of their last laugh lingering on her ear,
she turns to her needle, while the thousand memories
and hopes that make her being spring up in that mind-
leisure; now her voice breaks out into song, and now
a prayer nestles at her heart, soothing the thrilling
fear that *will* rise in the midst of a parent's most airy
visions.

The morning hours glided thus away as Mrs. Raymond sat in her shaded parlour. It was fresh and
laughing June; the earth was green as a Dryad's bower;
and white clouds rolled in fantastic beauty over the
mountains, the breath of roses was borne on the breeze,
and a few songsters hovered about the elms, whose
branches drooped in graceful arches over the portico.

The clock struck twelve, and soon the quick footsteps of Ruth Raymond were heard. Her cape-bonnet

was tossed aside, with spelling-book and grammar, that " Slough of Despond" to little people, and her pret-ty lips were pressed on her mother's.

" Who was that little boy I saw across the street as you came in, Ruth ?" said her mother.

Ruth stopped skipping a rope she had seized on en-tering, and said, " Willie White, mamma; he comes home *my* way. I'll tell you something if you will not tell *any*body."

The promise was given, and Ruth whispered in her mother's ear.

" I cannot hear a syllable, child," said her mother; " speak louder."

" But I am afraid you will *tell*, mamma," said Ruth, with a very conscious look, smoothing down her apron.

" Certainly I will not," said Mrs. Raymond ; " you may trust your own mother."

· Ruth looked round to ascertain if they were quite alone, and pressed her mouth so close to her mother's ear that the words were lost again.

Ruth made another effort. " Mind, mamma, you are not to tell anybody. Willie White is *my* sweet-heart."

" Who is Willie White ?" said her mother, smiling.

" I do not know, mamma," answered Ruth ; " but he has pretty curling hair, and a new hat, and comes *my* way from his school."

" How often have you seen Willie White ?" said Mrs. Raymond.

" A good many times, mamma," answered Ruth, be-ginning to skip her rope.

" You must not speak to strange boys," said Mrs. Raymond ; " it is not proper."

"I never speak to Willie White, mamma," said Ruth, with a pretty air of dignity. "He goes his side of the street, and I come mine. He said, *my* name is Willie White, and I said *my* name is Ruth Raymond. Just think, mamma, I have kept up the rope twenty times!"

Mrs. Raymond gazed admiringly on the child. Her round white arms thrown in unconsciously graceful attitudes, her small feet glancing here and there, her hair springing up and down, all betrayed the mere beauty of childhood; but as her mother caught a ray from her eyes, their mysterious beauty told of woman.

Some weeks passed away, and Ruth rushed in from school with sparkling eyes, exclaiming,

"Willie White has given me this pretty pink, mamma! How sweet it smells.. Will you have it?"

"Thank you, my darling," said Mrs. Raymond; "but you forget that I told you not to speak to strange boys."

"We did not speak, mamma," said Ruth, earnestly. "Willie just came half way across the street and held out the pink, and I went half way and took it. Willie has a nice new jacket on, and I have a new frock. Is not that funny? Will you go and see my anthills, mamma, and give me some sugar for the ants?"

Mrs. Raymond laid aside her book, and Ruth, taking her mother's hand, led her to the garden. Children are beautiful objects among flowers. There is something in their slight forms, their elastic tread, their lovely glow, that assimilates them to these delightful creations; we feel that they are heaven's blossoms. To her mother's eye, nothing was fairer amid the bloom than Ruth. She would almost have yielded to classic lore, and fancied the place peopled with airy beings peeping from tree and shrub to gaze upon the girl, had not a riper religion, a purer philosophy, turned her thoughts to a higher power.

· "Here are my pets working away," said Ruth, as she stopped and drew her mother's attention to two anthills, side by side. "Now, mamma, you will see how the little people will carry their load up hill." Then crumbling the sugar, she sprinkled it around, and as the ants began to remove their spoil, she clapped her hands and shouted aloud.

"Mamma," said she, speaking in a lower tone, "do you know what I call my anthills? This one I call Ruth, and that biggest one I call Willie White."

One day Ruth came home from school without her airy step and joyous voice, and her mother saw traces of tears on her face.

"What is the matter, my love?" said Mrs. Raymond.

"I *hate* William White," said Ruth; and her bright lips pouted in a crimson glow.

· "Ruth, my child, what language!" exclaimed her mother. "You must not hate any one."

"But I *will* hate William White," said Ruth, with a flushed brow and quivering lip. "Sally Swan says his curls look like a lapdog, and—and" (Mrs. Raymond could scarcely make out the rest of the sentence for her sobbing) "she says *I* have a lapdog for *my* sweetheart."

Willie White, imboldened by the acceptance of his pink, one morning selected the ripest bunch of cherries on his plate at breakfast and laid them aside.

"Who are those fine cherries for, Willie?" said his father.

Willie blushed up to the eyebrows, and said, "I

don't know, sir." It was his first untruth; the tempter begins early. Just as Willie came out of his door, Ruth's gate opened, and the little girl appeared. Willie coughed slightly. Ruth seemed very busy arranging her books. Willie held up the cherries with a smile; Ruth saw as though she saw not.

"Ruth, Ruth Raymond," said Willie, getting courage, "will you have these cherries?" Ruth raised her eyes kindly and hesitated; but in his zeal to reach her, Willie's cap fell off, and displayed his thick-clustering ringlets hanging bright in the sunbeams. A painter would have sacrificed a fortune for such a picture as Willie presented, when, with his frank, glowing face chastened by modesty, he held out the fruit. But that which would have given Michael Angelo a subject for a seraph brought to little Ruth only the appalling image of a lapdog, and with a half frightened look she hastened on, disregarding him.

Willie was surprised, but followed his young neighbour until he saw that her step was clearly an avoiding one. ·

"If Miss Ruth does not like cherries, I do," said he; and he philosophically ate them.

Thus the first pleasant dream of young love was broken; and ever after that, when Ruth knew that Willie was opposite, she looked straight forward, and the name of Willie White's anthill was changed to Mr. Perkins; a most vague and heartless baptism.

CHAPTER III.

The Naturalist.—Ruth's Prejudice.—The Cure.—Her Sense of Justice disturbed.—The Butterfly race.—Ruth's Danger.—Change of Feeling.—Doubts.

RUTH's attention was diverted from her " love passage" with Willie White by a letter of introduction to her father, announcing Dr. Gesner, a German, an enthusiastic entomologist, who visited the village to pursue his favourite studies in its beautiful retirement.

The naturalist, of course, dined early with the Raymonds. His broad face was deeply indented with the smallpox; his eyes, of a glassy blue, disclosed veins reddened by midnight study; his ears were huge, his hair crisp and unmanageable; he bore about him through the day the odour of onions from his morning meal, and an ocean of snuff lay upon his cravat and shirt bosom; he spoke the English imperfectly, and the saliva flew to a wonderful distance as he gave out his odd sentences; he talked a good deal of diet and dyspepsy, while laying on his fork for each mouthful a store for one delicate appetite.

As Ruth saw him load his fork and expand his shark-like mouth, her own opened instinctively, and, forgetting all things else, her head and jaws accompanied his movements.

Mrs. Raymond recalled her, by gently touching her foot under the table; but the sense of the ludicrous followed that of surprise, and Ruth glancing at her broth-

B 2

er, they began a giggle, that ended only by Ruth's being sent up stairs.

Yet it was not a week before Ruth was on the doctor's knee and by his side, in the true spirit of social
intercourse, for he loved childhood; his mouth seemed
to contract, the onion odour was softened, and thus was
one of her first prejudices overcome.

Nor was Ruth soon wearied as he unfolded to her
the beautiful and grand in nature, the nicety with which
the Creator has adjusted all his works, and how he
provides as bountifully for the insect that flutters in
summer sunshine as for rolling worlds.   And he soon
loved the fair creature, who ran across the meadow at
every leisure moment to visit his museum, to look
through his microscope at the cable-like legs of spi-
ders, and feel natural disgust give way before deep
admiration of the vast and wonderful in the machinery
of insect life.   But the butterfly creation was her delight.   How often had she expended her strength in
fruitless chases over garden and meadow for them,
and sitten down panting and exhausted as they eluded
her grasp; now their gorgeous outspread wings, arrested in their ephemeral career, were all before her.

So far all was well; but, unfortunately, Ruth burst
into the doctor's room on one occasion, when he was
about to impale a butterfly which, for size and richness,
seemed the very prince of his tribe.   Ruth, eager and
delighted at first, soon sided with the weaker party.
She pleaded for his release, as the naturalist's huge
fingers daintily touched the velvet wings, that none of
its exquisite down might be removed, while with the
right hand he balanced a fine, sharp needle.   Too in-
tent on his prize to regard Ruth's countenance, he saw

not the tears gathering in her eyes as the needle was inserted, and the graceful wings of the prisoner first fluttered in agitation, then flapped slowly, then stiffened in death. Ruth's feelings grew and swelled, and rushing from the spot, she vowed that she would never enter it again. It was hard to say whether grief or indignation was most prominent, as she flew to her mother and related the occurrence; but at length the tears left her eyes, though her cheeks were wet, and indignation remained.

"An old, dirty, snuff-taking onion-eater!" said she; "I wish he may be stuck on a needle as thick as our spit, and six yards long!"

"Ruth, Ruth," said her mother, sternly, "you forget that you are as cruel now as you think Dr. Gesner to be. Go to your room and compose yourself."

Ruth went, and the principle of *justice* began to stir her young thoughts, the most difficult subject, perhaps, in the world, whether we connect it with the high dealings of the Creator, or with the feeble agents of his power.

A few days after this scene Ruth strolled to the foot of the garden, where a rustic bridge led to a mill, and stood amid a perfect gush of sunset glory. She seemed to muse, but I doubt if, at ten years of age, the aspect of natural beauty operates sensibly on the mind. The glowing sky, the vivid green of the hills and meadows, the hum of insects, the soft glitter of the trickling stream, and the stronger shout of falling waters, the whole rich apparatus of declining day, what are they like to early childhood but the colouring of ribands, the toys of the baby house? The key of experience must unlock the associations that give grace and power to natural beauty.

What were Ruth's thoughts as she seemed to muse on the rustic bridge over that pure stream, surrounded by a sunset that would have bathed Titian's soul in glory? Scarcely on aught but the leaves and small sticks gathering about the little whirlpool made by the mill. But a rustling on the bank aroused her, and, looking up, she espied Doctor Gesner panting and puffing, his broad-brimmed hat in his extended hand, ready to strike down a butterfly, which flitted bright, as if it were formed of the glowing clouds around, on its unconscious way.

Ruth darted to the bank to rescue the fugitive, and waved her handkerchief to expedite its flight.

"Oh, ho, you little puss!" shouted the doctor, "you scare my papilio, what you call butterfly. I keep one ver comfortable place for him in te glass cases, you know, mid de species Equites. Softly, puss!" vociferated the doctor, clapping his hand to his forehead and stamping in anxiety, as Ruth continued to wave her handkerchief. Then applying his eyeglass, as he approached the insect resting on a flower, he mumbled over the technical terms, "Asterias, wing-tailed, black, two macular bands, tail fulvous, &c. &c. Ho, the beauty! Eh, puss?" and then raising his hat, he stood prepared for a certain blow.

"You wicked man!" exclaimed Ruth, indignantly, forgetting all respect in her excitement; "you sha'n't kill him. I wish you may have forty needles stuck through you. I do."

It is probable that the German may not have understood Ruth's words, but her actions were unequivocal.

She rushed towards the flower. Starting together again along the bank of the stream, the trio kept the victory for some time doubtful, the doctor's long strides amply making up for Ruth's more youthful elasticity. Sometimes the butterfly turned back or stopped to sip a flower, and the guttural exclamations of the naturalist sounded in triumph, while his tiptoe step was more cautious, and his hat was depressed among the bushes ; then, as the fickle insect again took wing, Ruth clapped her hands, and laughed and shouted aloud.

The pursuers were now about equally distant, when the rover sought a neighbouring shrub. Ruth sprang forward, but her pocket handkerchief, her main weapon, was caught by the branch of a tree. While she was disengaging it, the doctor trod cautiously forward —one, two, three steps, and he was at the spot ; whang went the hat, and the beautiful flutterer fell to the ground. Ruth ran to the rescue, but, just as she reached him, her foot slipped, and she was precipitated into the stream.

I must do the doctor the justice to say, that he cast but *one* forlorn look on the insect as it struggled from underneath the hat and soared away, with its gay wings simply ruffled by the encounter, before he threw off his coat and dashed like a porpoise into the water.

The struggle was violent, for the current set strongly towards the mill, and our sweet child of love and hope would have passed away like a dream, had not the energy and presence of mind of the naturalist been wisely exerted. Catching her floating dress, he directed his course to the most sloping part of the bank, and, after many struggles, drew her towards the shore.

Ruth had sufficient instinct and perception to catch

at a shrub which bent towards the stream, and thus at-
tain a point of safety ; but what was her terror when
she perceived her preserver, in attempting to rise, stag-
ger back fainting into the water! A shrill, wild scream
brought two men to the spot before it was too late.
They rescued the doctor, and bore him to Mr. Raymond's. It was many days before he was restored to
entire consciousness. Ruth sat by his bedside with a
pitying look, or laid a fresh blossom on his pillow,
or sang hymns to sooth him ; and when he recovered,
her arms were round his neck, and her heart in his
bosom.

" Oh, ho, puss !" said the doctor one day as she caressed him, " somesing was turn your brain to make
me loss my papilio, what you call butterfly."

Ruth hung down her head, and that night again un-
settled thoughts of justice, undefined and disturbing,
oppressed her as she nestled on her pillow. She pit-
ied the butterflies, but she loved the good doctor who
had saved her life, and the morning sun awoke her to
a knowledge of good and evil.

CHAPTER IV.

Dancing.—Monsieur Lagrande.—Right Appreciation of Motives.—
Ruth's Dancing.—Her second Preference.—An awkward Predicament.—A Change.

So Ruth must go to dancing-school to the French
gentleman who has opened an untenanted shop in the
village, and called it a saloon.

Whatever judgment may be passed upon dancing as
an amusement for the serious and mature, every one
must allow its adaptedness to childhood. We all love
the active motions of youth; how agreeable is it to
see those motions modulated by music, touched by the
sentiment of sound. A dancing child is like a bright
rose-tree waved by a breeze.

Many persons have been surprised at the solemn and
affecting thanksgiving offered by Mrs. Siddons, the ac-
tress, when she learned, after her wonderful persona-
tion of the statue in the Winter's Tale, that her train
of tissue had caught on fire, and been extinguished
without her knowledge. Others have been surprised
at 'the declaration of the celebrated Mrs. Hamilton,
authoress of Treatise on Education, that the most religious moment of her whole life occurred in a ballroom. So, many persons may be astonished that a
dancing-master should teach on principle. When Mrs.
Raymond presented her blooming Ruth, with new kid
slippers and a pretty pink sash, to Monsieur Lagrande
at his saloon, he laid his hand upon his heart and said,

"Believe me, madame, Providence was bring me

through peril of much waters, to teach true grace to de nation Americane."

And, after an elaborate account of his system of instruction, he pressed the point of his fiddle-bow gently, but impressively, on Mrs. Raymond's arm, exclaiming,

"It is not all personne, madame, can teach de art of dance. It is one gift. For me, I am ordained for such office, what you call an apostle of dance," and he looked upward with an air of responsibility.

Let us who sneer at this apparent presumption beware lest a narrow and unphilosophic principle engender the sneer. Let us respect even a conscientious pirouette!

It was but little labour to teach Ruth to dance. Her flexible form melted to the music like a snow-flake on the wave; the harmony and she seemed to become one. I could never tell whether a certain expression about her were a consciousness of excelling, or the mere joy of motion, as she floated on with a birdlike sway, her head slightly inclined to one side, her eyes cast down, and a half smile on her lips. I wish I could say it was always thus with Ruth; I wish that budding child had unfolded every leaf with patient smoothness; but alas, when the wrong partner asked her for the dance, the rose-leaf was ruffled, a shade crossed her sunny brow like the changing hues of her own hills, while a sullen, pouting lip, and an uncourteous withdrawal of her hand, spoke volumes. Oh, Ruth! Ruth! this may be accounted for in the spoiled belle of sixteen, but you of eleven, was it thus with you?

And why was it that, when that youth you called

Frederic advanced with a bow like the bows of other boys, with gloves no fresher, shoes no blacker, and face no handsomer, your eye gleamed with a joyous acquiescence as you joined the dance like a feather on the breeze ?

Ruth never asked herself this question, nor did she know the *why*. Who does ? Where and what is the charm that speaks from eye to eye, and says we understand each other ? Even the infant has its preferences. Carry one among a group of strangers, and you will see the grieved lip show alarm and disgust at some, while to others the young disciple of human feeling stretches out its arms in wooing confidence.

Frederic was evidently the favourite of Ruth ; as for Willie White, he danced in another set with a Miss Rhoda something. But the strength of Ruth's new preference remained to be tested. As she was gliding along in the mazes of a quadrille, her foot slipped, and she fell prostrate, not in the graceful position which makes even a fall beautiful, but flat on her back. She scrambled up, and heard among the laughter one well-known note prolonged and louder than the rest. It was Frederic's. With mixed emotions of anger and shame she burst into tears, and, on recovering, whispered to a little girl near her,

" I don't like that old Frederic !"

In ten minutes her hand was given to a tall, shuffling boy with slouching shoulders, at whom she had often jested, and bright was the angry glow on her cheek which dried her lingering tears, and tremulous the voice which said,

" Don't you think Frederic Maxwell ought to be

C

ashamed to laugh? If he gets down on his knees to me I won't dance with him."

Fortunately for Ruth's resolution, it was the last week of the quarter. Monsieur Lagrande departed to enlighten the heels of another coterie, and Frederic went to a distant academy.

CHAPTER V.

Ruth's Singing.—A Mother's Mistake.—A Question about Birds.—
Ruth falls into Extremes.—A Glimpse at the Future.—Angel
Choirs.

" Is that Ruth singing ?" said some morning guests
to Mrs. Raymond, as the child, unconscious as a bird,
sat at the door-sill watching a dissolving icicle dripping
from the eaves of the piazza. " Pray let us hear her
sing."

Mrs. Raymond felt a slight struggle between good
sense and vanity, but the latter unfortunately triumphed, for she unduly valued Ruth's childish warble and
simple hymns.

Do birds recognise and prize the notes of their fledg-
lings, when, released from their nests, they blend their
songs with the harmony of nature ?   I have sometimes
thought of this when the feathered choir have been up
and awake amid the branches of a summer forest.   Be
this as it may, Mrs. Raymond enjoyed the first warb-
lings of *her* singing-bird with maternal fondness.

" Ruth, love," said she, as the child bounded in, "the
ladies wish to hear you sing."

Ruth blushed and almost retreated, but a gently in-
sisting look brought her forward.

" Come, Ruth," said her mother, " you were singing
' The Mellow Horn.'   Imagine yourself quite alouc'ou
the door-step again, and sing it for us."

Vain request !   Ruth felt herself in the presence of
strangers without *love*, and their heedful eyes disturbed

her. Nerving herself, however, for the trial, she stood
stiffly before her mother, and with her hands clasped
in front, her face losing all its sweet mobility, began.
She had proceeded but a few notes before discovering
that the pitch was too high, and, not having self-com-
mand to stop and recommence, endeavoured to aid
herself by straining her neck and rising on tiptoe.
These instinctive movements failed to help her out;
her face reddened, her veins swelled, and the chorus
came out in an attenuated squeak.

"A little lower, my love," said Mrs. Raymond, who
had been gradually elevating her own head, and lifting
her own feet in sympathy with Ruth; "take the pitch
a little lower, dear."

Poor Ruth began louder, but not lower, and the
"Mellow Horn" was anything but mellow.

Mrs. Raymond, but too sensible of the difficulty,
caught her breath, and suggested "Away with Melancholy" as better adapted to her voice. Ruth looked
imploringly, but the ladies exclaimed, "Oh yes, Away
with Melancholy; sing that, dear; it is very low!"

And low it was. Ruth took a note as deep

"As the Domdaniel caves
At the root of the ocean,"

and having reached

"Nor doleful changes ring,"

came to a sudden halt, with a perplexed look, and
caught a glimpse of one of the ladies diligently stuffing
her handkerchief into her mouth.

Mrs. Raymond wisely patted the little girl on the
head, and told her to go and play. And Ruth, the water standing in her eyes from physical exertion, gladly
retreated, to seek companionship with nature, and send

her wild notes on the winds. There unseen hands tuned her spirit's harp; the harp whose tones in after years were to tranquillize, to elevate, or inspire, as the mood of the songster changed from grave to gay; that harp which was destined to lead the soul to heaven in sacred song, to marry immortal verse to harmony, and to waken love's chastest aspirations.

What spiritual eyes were gazing from above on that unconscious one? What group, what celestial choir then began to form, in which her voice should chime immortally? What if she even heard them as she hurried to the green spot where the spring-sun dwelt on the first snowdrop, and looked upward as if listening to some pleasant sound?

That evening Ruth sat by her mother's side, on her father's knee; no word was said of the morning, but her voice rose sweet and clear, for *love* was her impulse and her reward.

C 2

CHAPTER VI.

Young Things.—Ruth too old for Dolls.—The Doll Family.—A Letter.—Ruth's Favourite.—A solemn Conclusion.

READER, if you do not love young things, turn away-
from this chapter, for Ruth and I are going to take a
look into her baby-house. It is the last look, but we
shall give ourselves up to it with *gusto*; besides, we are
somewhat tired of grown-up things. Our ancient cat
is lazy; our flowers have gone to seed and smell musty; the apples on that old mossy tree are sour; that
peach-tree has outlived its time, and become wormy;
the old stone wall is tumbling over; the town clock is
almost too infirm to strike; the old cow has dried up;
the mare is broken down; the old man opposite proses,
the old lady has no teeth, and we ourselves are getting
gray.

But look now at young things, at that kitten, for instance; did you ever see anything like her vivacity and
grace as she chases her own tail, until a somerset brings
her to her senses? See these rosebuds, fresh, exquisite,
opening with such a gush of beauty that I catch my
breath for joy. Look at this apple-tree, with its graft-
ed fruit, ruddy, ripe, like a young girl's cheek. Let
us taste a nectarine from this young tree; U-i-p, I can
scarcely speak for its juicy fulness as I break the
glowing skin. Observe our new stone wall, how level
and neat; the very squirrels are baffled by its com-
pactness; hear the clock on the new opposition church;

one, two, three! how clear and young it sounds! Just
sip a bowl of milk from our new cow; it looks like a
draught of melted pearl; and here is Tibbet, the broken colt. Mount him; he has no tricks, though he is
young; he will carry you as smooth as a railroad.
Eh! here is a young man too. What lustrous dark
eyes, what supple limbs! Tall and bending as the
osier, he has leaped the wall for mere pastime; and lo,
yonder approaches a young maiden, bright as a rose
and fresh as a lily; the very breeze rejoices to play
with her fair hair. See her springing step; she and
the young man have met. Mercy on my old eyes!
Betsy, is it you? You had better go home, my dear.

*   *   *   *   *

"Ruth, you are twelve years old," said her mother,
gravely, "and it is time for you to give up your dolls.
You are really too childish. Your little cousins are
coming to see you, and you must give *them* your toys."

Ruth stood thoughtfully looking at her baby-house,
and every article seemed to assume a new value; for,
though in the waning stage of doll-ism, and except on
rainy days almost weaned, yet now her old love revi-
ved. On holydays she always commenced what she
called a *thorough fixing*, which fixing ended in a general overturn of her whole establishment, and she had
just begun to upset everything with great zeal. Much
has been said of the advantage of dolls in teaching
girls to sew; I cannot class my little Ruth in the rank
of those who improved in this department under the
reign of doll-ism. Her needle took tremendous licen-
ses, while nondescript caps and bonnets grew under
her scissors; but her heart received better lessons.
She was surrounded by a world of her own, fanciful I

know, but still a world dependant on her, and this feeling of superiority is one deep fountain of love.

There is a peculiar air of helplessness about the inmates of a neglected baby-house that almost excites compassion. Scarcely a doll stands erect; they lean, and tumble, and stride, or they are flat on their backs looking up at the ceiling, or on their faces helpless, prone, and take many attitudes painful to the lovers of doll-like etiquette in their odd proximities.

It was on such a scene as this that Ruth now gazed, and it was in this predicament her dolls had been left after the last rainy day. The only figure that preserved its propriety was a large wax doll from New-York, scarcely injured by time, with its bright blue eyes, flaxen hair, and tinsel dress. Her cognomen was Miss Butterfly. Beside her lay the dancing doll, a purchase from a fair; it had passed its ephemeral hour of triumph, and now bore a broken leg, an affecting lesson on all such skipping propensities. Then there was a large stuffed baby, the antipode of the flat-backed dancer, whose redundant cotton materials oozed out at every pore; there were some without legs, the squatters, or, perchance, fakirs of the doll tribe, and others who seemed to have made the vow never to sit. Here might be seen a head bald as if from the scalping-knife; and there were wigs as changeable in hue as that of a celebrated senator facetiously described by an English lady. There was the once stiff-bodied kid doll, dangling and dropping sawdust at every movement of its flaccid limbs; there were bodies without heads, and heads without bodies; a bloodless massacre of the innocents. In one corner was a bedstead too small for its occupants, showing that Ruth was no Procrustéan; for, hanging from under its scanty covering,

> "Some saw a hand, and some an arm,
> And some the waving of a gown."

Then there were painted dolls of all sizes classed in families; among them the three Miss Derbys and their mamma, who had accidentally lost her face. It had pealed off, leaving a white limy surface, on which Ruth had drawn features with a pen; features by which the Miss Derbys could never have recognised their respectable parent. Then there were nondescript little things made of rags, with inked faces. It was the completion of one of these that brought forth Ruth's first pun, who ran shouting to her mother, "A doll I try," which pun Mrs. Raymond was apt to repeat until it was somewhat stale.

Besides this infantile regiment, Ruth was in the habit of taking dolls to board at a pin a week. Pinned to the hand of one Mrs. Raymond found the following epistle:

"Dear mamma, i am well and hope you are the same. i like to board with Miss Ruth there is twenty five dolls of us counting the one without a head which stays on the shelf. i don't like the Miss Derbys, they are so proud one of them spit on me. We have a very serious family, i like a serious family, nobody laughs but Miss Ruth. Two of Miss Ruth's dolls is to be married. Dr. Gesner is to be the marrier. Mr. Washington Irving is to marry Miss Hannah More, and Miss Beauty is to be bridemaid.

"The marrying is done. Mr. Irving had new clothes and Miss Hannah More put on a veil. Dr.

Gesner kissed the dolls and said now you are married, and we all laughed except the Miss Derbys and they spit. I am your dutyful daughter,

"NANCY DOLL.

"Miss Ruth says you owe a pin for last week's board, and if you don't pay she shall sew you."

Mrs. Raymond, who rightly attributed this epistle to Ruth, was shocked, as well she might be, with its inaccuracy, particularly with the want of capital I's.

The Miss Beauty, a doll without a nose, alluded to as bridemaid, was Ruth's favourite. It had been her companion for so long a period that it seemed a part of her, and she devotedly loved this fright, with its blear eyes and leprous-looking complexion. This was the doll she had talked to ; to this she had fitted garments, and this she caressed on her pillow. While the elegant Miss Butterfly sat in a state unnoticed and unloved, Ruth's low or gladsome song was poured out over Miss Beauty's faded form. Sometimes she was even jealous of the dashing New-Yorker.

"You think yourself very grand, Miss Butterfly," said she, as the unconscious image sat upright, glaring at her with its blue eyes, "you think yourself very grand because you have a smart frock, and red cheeks, and curling hair, but I love poor Beauty better with her old face ; don't I, Beauty ?" and she bestowed a kiss on the jagged cheeks of her favourite.

It was with a feeling of peculiar tenderness then that Ruth glanced at Miss Beauty, who now sat with her face to the wall, one foot resting on the shoulder of another of the fraternity. Her cousins came, and she gracefully distributed her little store among them ;

but Beauty was quietly withdrawn and placed in a drawer. It was a silent but emphatic triumph of *Love*. That soiled, marred, disfigured image, which she laid apart in tender sadness, what was it but an emblem full of deep meaning? It lay alone and in darkness; it was ridiculed, but she cherished it still.

And so, Ruth, we have seen you sunder your first juvenile associations. The toys of *infancy* are scattered, the baby-house is closed. By-and-by the toys of *girlhood* will be thrown away. After that will come the last great change; you will lie down in the grave, and the broken toys of earth too will vanish.

CHAPTER VII.

The Sleep of Childhood.—Its Terrors.—A Story from Dr. Gesner.
—Ruth's Distress.—Its Cure.

PAINTERS have sketched and poets have sung the sleep of childhood. The contrast of Ruth's sleep with her waking was lovely, In her day face there was a restless, flashing charm, which took the gazer by a sweet surprise, and an undulation, a wave in her motions, that conveyed an instantaneous thought of life; but her repose was statue-like; sleep took possession of her like an enchantress, and her white night-dress lay still as chiselled marble on her bosom. But who can tell the wild and fearful thoughts that preceded this profound repose? None but those who, like Ruth, have trembled at the mystery of darkness, and many such there are, for no innocence shuts out this terrible visitation from childhood. The gallant boy, who over-comes difficulties and assails foes in sunshine, cowers with a throbbing heart on his pillow; and many a young girl, conversant through the day with sights and sounds of gladness, from which one would think her after thoughts would take their colour, glances fearfully through her apartment, hurries over her prayers, and covers up her eyes with the bedclothes, her head al-most glued to her pillow in its nervous pressure.

As yet the discipline of Ruth's parents had been un-availing to conquer her fear of loneliness at night. The signal for rest was to her like a call to a prison.

· One evening, the closing meal of the day was over, the fire blazed brightly, some pleasant neighbours entered, and the little circle, gradually laying aside books and work, gathered around the hearth, and fell into those discussions on supernatural appearances to which the mind insensibly turns from its every-day experience. Each had some anecdote to tell or theory to urge ; and as Ruth sat on her low seat by Dr. Gesner's knee, drinking in the discourse with eager curiosity, he smoothed down her hair with his great hand, and related his experience too.

" My habits as a naturalist," he said, " have led me into many adventures. Being on a pedestrian excursion, I was once overtaken by night in an unfrequented part of my own country, and, while doubtful which way to turn, a storm arose, increasing the wildness of the scene and the perplexity of my feelings. The rain fell in torrents, the lightning glared fiercely, and the thunder went rattling on from cloud to cloud like the war-chariots of the gods. I groped my way from tree to tree, totally uncertain which way to bend my course. As I approached one, a flash of lightning rent it from its topmost bough to the solid trunk, and the electric fluid rushed over me, bringing a momentary suspension of my faculties. On recovering, I passed the tree ; its shivered splinters were revealed by the lightning, standing out in bent and jagged twistings. I hurried on by a kind of impulse, as if the ghost of the stricken tree could pursue me, until another flash of lightning revealed to me a solitary building. I was not slow in hastening to its shelter. There appeared to be only one room, with a low, unsashed window, protected from the elements by a shed without. Groping around

D

the apartment, I felt some straw, seemingly thrown for
a bed, beneath the window, and, finding no occupant,
took off my dripping garments, clothed myself afresh
from my knapsack, and laid down on the straw. Grateful for the shelter, I soon fell asleep, and dreamed
that I was chasing a huge dragon-fly. My happy and
profound rest was broken just before day by a sound
near me of such strange and terrific power, that I
thought a legion of fiends had assailed me; a sound
accompanied with a blow on my face. I listened in
terror. It was repeated, but fierce and deep breathing
sounded close to my ear. Though bewildered with
my deep sleep, I resolved to meet my fate with bra-
very; and aiming with both hands at the object over
me, caught hold of a mass of long, flowing hair.
'Speak,' said I, sternly, 'if you have the spark of
man's spirit about you, who are you, and what do you
want with an unoffending traveller?' There was no reply, but a kind of moan, a tremendous thrust at the
wainscot outside, the same breath of awful and por-
tentous power, and the low growl of the departing
thunder.

  " I kept my hands clutched to the hair, resolved not
to give up my advantage, trusting to my unusual mus-
cular strength, until the dawning day should reveal my
foe, while thoughts of assassins were but too busy in
my agitated brain. Once more I appealed to my prisoner.

  "'Speak, man, or whatever you are,' I said, 'speak.
I am but a poor traveller. I have no gold, no silver.
Two dragon-flies, five lizards in bottles, and a frog of
a new species, which I hope some Society of Natural-
ists will name for me, are all my possessions.'

" The assassin muttered and jerked, but returned no answer. Fortunately for me, for the joints of my fingers were becoming stiff by long effort, the day began to dawn. I looked with strained and eager sight to my prisoner, and discovered, not the terrible murderer I feared, but the tail of a donkey protruded through the window.

" You laugh, my beauty," said the doctor, who had told his story in his broken English ; " but if somesing was flap in your face in se darkness, you scare too, Miss Ruth."

Amid the laughter and frolic occasioned by the doctor's story, Ruth was dismissed for the night unusually excited ; the bright lights, the affectionate caress, all forming but too strong a contrast to her lonely room. Darkness and silence soon peopled her imagination with unreal shapes. Conscious of her own weakness and of her parents' resolution to conquer it, she struggled with her feelings and went to bed. She had no sooner tried to close her eyes, than the little circles of light retained on the retina seemed to increase to such a frightful number as if space could not contain them ; then they danced off to a distance, then crowded near, until she felt suffocated, and threw off the bedclothes in terror. Sleep fled away ; and, starting up in bed, she strained her eyes open, when some new imagination, rising in the darkness, made her crouch down again and crush her lids together, until the physical effort was painful. She heard the cheerful voices below ; they seemed a mockery of her sufferings ; and with irresistible impulse, she screamed, " Mother, mother."

Mrs. Raymond came to her, remonstrated, scolded, soothed, *and left her.* Ruth remained a few moments silent, but she wept bitterly, and felt like an outcast; she could not be still; and, rising softly, stole down stairs and sat at the foot, where she could hear *human words*. Mr. Raymond found her there, and told her angrily to retire. She went, and thought him hard-hearted. Alas, she did not know that her parents, bewildered and sorrowful, sat almost in tears by her door. Again she screamed, "Father, mother." Mr. Raymond entered her room and chastised her. Ruth, terrified and ashamed, wept bitterly, again said her prayers, repeated her multiplication table, and at last wept herself to sleep. She did not know that an hour afterward her father was bending over her now placid sleep in love and prayer.

The next night, and the next, and the next, the poor trembler crouched down in silence, conquered in body but not in mind. Fear of man will rarely triumph over the imagination; the dread of darkness and loneliness usually masters every other. The banished child will feel her best friends to be her enemies, if no trusting love nestles on her pillow. I am filled with a deep sentiment of melancholy when I contemplate the sufferings of a timid child. Parents, guardians, mould them with *love*. They are delicate plants that turn to you for life and nourishment; why let their sunny time be overcast with fear?

"Suppose," said Mrs. Raymond, soon after this event, "we let Ruth sleep with her sister."

It acted like a charm. Companionship drove out fear; sympathy, *love* was called forth, and Ruth, with her arm around her sister's neck, sank to rest like a summer blossom.

CHAPTER VIII.

Ruth not a Genius.—The promised Prize at School.—Dangers of the
System.—Effect on Ruth.—Ruth's Triumph.—The Exhibition.— ⟩
Abby Mansfield.— Ruth's Mortification and Self-Conquest.—The
Prize awarded.

RUTH had never been what is called a genius. Up to
the age of twelve she had learned her lessons mechanically. Dates were her stumbling-block, and were
totally unaccompanied by ideas. She was aided in her
lessons and recitations by Abby Mansfield, a bright, per-
severing girl, who had long sustained the first place in
the class without a rival. When Ruth was in her thir-
teenth year, it was announced that a public examination would take place at the usual time, on which occasion a prize would be given, and the best scholar
crowned with a wreath of flowers. Ruth suddenly
awoke, and rushed to her books with a diligence and
thoroughness that astonished the school. Thought was
busy on her brow, her mental energy expanded, and
with it a consciousness of her power. But the process with her heart and affections was less favourable,
for she was a rival to Abby Mansfield. The plan of
school prizes is one always attended with heart-burn-
ing. There should either be no prize, or else so many
and so graduated, that every scholar who has any merit
either of the head or heart (and who has not some?)
should carry home a little testimonial to prevent the
almost infinite distance between the *prize* and none.
How many fine minds are depressed by the almost in-

vidious distinction springing from prizes, and then how
many wild and bad passions are let loose! How much
cunning and envy enter on the arena of a school thus
constituted!

A book was kept by Miss Southward, the teacher,
and a mark placed against the name of those who were
at the head of their class at the close of a recitation.
She who obtained the most was to win the prize. The
first day Ruth attained this enviable situation was in
the absence of Abby, who was detained at home by indisposition. A thrill of exultation ran through her
whole frame, crushing the soft and tender sympathy that
had bound her so long to her friend. From that moment she allowed herself no respite from study until
her tasks were accomplished. Abby pursued her
course in calm self-possession, while Ruth was now wild
with gayety, and then depressed, cold, and thoughtful.
Sometimes, as she saw the fluctuating scale of marks,
an awfully dark temptation crossed her thoughts, which
she repulsed with self-disgust.

"Oh, Abby," she said often, "if there were only two
prizes!"

Abby smiled kindly. "I wish there were," said she;
"but I am willing this should be yours."

One day Ruth rushed home glowing and triumphant.
"I have more marks than Abby, mamma; I shall have
the prize!"

"But poor Abby!" said her mother.

"I know it," said Ruth, despondingly. "Sometimes
I feel wicked, mamma, when I think of that prize."

Mrs. Raymond was silent; it was her habit to let a
good impulse have its way.

The few remaining weeks flew by, and Ruth still

maintained her slight though decided ascendency. Her manners to Abby, though affectionate, were deficient in that rush of confidence where sympathy is perfect.

The day of exhibition arrived. A formidable circle was placed in regular arrangement around the apartment; while the pupils, dressed in white, the classes distinguished by sashes of different colour, sat on each side and behind their teacher, who presided at a table on which was placed a box containing the prize and wreath.

Ruth, who was at the head of the class, flushed and agitated, stumbled on the very threshold, and shunned the gaze of the expectant audience. Dates, her old trial, were sadly *anachronized*, and at last, after stammering a while on the most simple proposition, the tears rolled from her eyes, and she stopped short. Abby softly prompted, and then endeavoured to screen her, but to no good effect ; the tears fairly rolled down, and self-possession was gone. Her friend, well grounded in all her studies, recited with the air of one to whom knowledge was familiar; her voice, full of sweet distinctness, conveyed all that her teacher wished should be understood, while a gentle glow lit up her placid face with spiritual beauty.

As Ruth listened to her beautiful recitation, a thoughtful mood came over her, which gradually strengthened to an air of determination ; then a bright agitation kindled in her eye and burned on her cheek ; and when the class was dismissed to give place to another, she softly stole behind her teacher's chair.

"Miss Southward," whispered she, while a deeper flush rose even to her brow, " I do not deserve the prize, and I shall feel miserable if Abby does not receive it.

I have exerted myself for a few months, and she has been your best scholar for years."

Miss Southward smiled kindly. " Your generous feelings shall be consulted. I have watched you both with great interest, Ruth." And she pressed Ruth's hand as it rested on the back of her chair.

Ruth breathed more freely.

" Who is that exquisite creature," said a lady to Miss Southward, " who just spoke to you, with such a rainbow struggle between tears and smiles ?"

The exercises were concluded, and there was the usual hush over the audience, when Miss Southward rose and called " Miss Ruth Raymond."

Ruth started, blushed, and shrank back, but an imperative look from her teacher brought her forward; and Miss Southward threw a medal round her neck, and placed a wreath of flowers in her hair.

" My dear Ruth," she said aloud, " as my plan will not permit *me* to bestow two prizes, I authorize you to dispose of this as you will."

Saying this, she drew from the box another medal and wreath, and laid them in Ruth's hand. Ruth sprang to her friend, gladly and proudly threw the medal on her neck, and placed the crown on her brow, while the two, tearful, blushing, and smiling, stood together, touching monuments of childhood's *love*.

CHAPTER IX.

Friendship's first Grief.—The new Friend.—Patronage and Love.—
First reading of Shakspeare.—The Kitten Perdita's Danger.—Its
Rescue.

WHY is Ruth sorrowful? She has stolen from the
family circle, retreated to her own apartment, and taken from her escrutoire a love-knot of soft brown hair,
which lies within a larkspur wreath, tied with blue
riband. She has gazed on it sadly and sighed. Why
is Ruth Raymond sorrowful? Abby Mansfield has
chosen another bosom-friend. A classmate of her
father's has brought his daughter to the village, and
they are seen arm interlacing arm, earnest looks and
significant smiles pass between them, and they are
whispering those whispers that Abby once shared with
Ruth only. They have just gone by the gate with
laughter, and Ruth heard their voices as she sat alone
in the garden, and saw their white dresses as they
passed down the green lane to that very moss-grown
stone which Ruth thought was consecrated to her.

Ruth shook her head thoughtfully as she replaced
the little relic of friendship, and said almost aloud,

" Let her go, if she will. I would not have deserted *her* for a stranger."

And then, with a step bereft of its elastic spring, she
descended the stairs. When near the foot she heard
a shout in the piazza, and soon perceived a dirty, trembling kitten, followed by the children, who kicked or
shrank from it with exclamations of disgust. Ruth

instantly took it under her protection, warded off the boys, and, finding none of the servants willing to attempt its ablution, undertook herself such a process of purification as was given to Tom Jones in the house of Mr. Allworthy. If the kitten had been comely, one might have thought it a reward for her benevolence ; but the streams of Fair Mount would not have had power to change the undefined gray of her coat, nor could all Ruth's training lend an air of feline aristocracy to the poor little stranger. But *love* soon began to work in Ruth's heart, or pity, which is akin to love, inspiring an emotion which the sleek, well-fed cat of the household had never obtained from her. Ruth had commenced Shakspeare, and her pet was appropriately named Perdita. It was soothing to her, now that she experienced the first grief of *forsakenness*, to listen to her kitten's soft breathings, or watch her noiseless tread from room to room, or caress her as the little puss

"With soft insinuating purr
"Brush'd by her ankle with her silken fur."

The principle of *love,* to the development of which my story leads, seems to be an attachment to something existing apart from purely natural relations ; a something which even the filial and fraternal bond cannot supply. It may be the beginning of that restlessness which signs us as immortal, but it is often lavished on most insignificant objects. Cowper was full of this out-of-door tenderness, and his rabbits have become themes for biography. Byron, maddening against the world, petted a bear ; while the countless parrots, tabbies, lap-dogs, and canaries, which receive the lavish tenderness of the happy and the sad, show that there

is something in the breast which mere consanguinity
cannot supply.   Thus, when Ruth found a void in her
heart, it was not filled up by her brothers and sisters,
though they were a winning set of little urchins, but
she beguiled herself with Perdita.   Glorious were the
frolics of those two; the racing, and climbing, and tumbling over, until quieter hours came, when the kitten
nestled in the lap of her protector, looking gratitude !
Ruth had frowned and scolded down all ridicule of her
darling, and her only fear was from a circle of youths,
who assembled together, under a lecturer on chemistry, in the village.   Dark rumours went abroad that
the feline community were but too often immolated by
them on the shrine of science.   Ruth shuddered as
she listened to the tales of these Torricellian bandits,
and clasped her little Perdita closer in her arms.

I have said that Ruth was reading Shakspeare.   Oh
that first delicious opening of the mental firmament,
when *his* beams look through to enlighten and to bless !

Ruth's tasks were over for the day.   The stale and
musty road of History had been trodden, the eternal
Jingle of the piano was hushed, and, with book in hand,
she retired to the garden, forgetting even Perdita.   But
Perdita would not be forgotten; she well knew where
Ruth would be, and hastened after her with reproachful mewings.   There was an apple-tree by the garden
wall, on a limb of which was Ruth's favourite seat.
It was so low that a stone was her footstool, while her
back rested against the body of the tree, a branch of
which screened her from the lane.   I wish I could
paint this bright expanding girl at that very hour, her
white hand glittering through the foliage, as her arm
entwined the tree, one foot swinging easily, while the

other rested on the stone! But I am partial to Ruth, and may overcharge the picture. The scene around her was worthy of her; mountain and river, blossoms and the skies! and Perdita too helped out the picture, as she frisked on the gravelled paths below.

It was Shakspeare's Tempest that Ruth now opened. She glanced at the Dramatis Personæ, and from that to the kitten, which was chasing a dead leaf which a little local whirling wind was carrying along. Ruth cheered on her pet, the leaf was attained, then slighted, and she sat looking up in Ruth's face silently.

Ruth began,

" Master. Boatswain !

" Boats. Here, master; what cheer?"

Perdita started, and then crouched down ready to spring on a butterfly, which, hovering over an evening primrose, seemed to wait its first opening.

" You little monster," said Ruth, waving off the insect, " you are after the papilio, what you call butterfly, eh?"

Perdita yielded to her loss with all kittenly meekness, and purred herself to sleep, while Ruth read on.

And now the scene began to change; she no longer sat on the old apple-tree amid the garden bloom; the Hudson glided not on its smooth way; the mist rose not amid the hills; the robin's note was unheard. She was on a desert island; the heavens were darkened; thunders rolled and lightning gleamed on the clashing clouds; a solitary ship was seen toiling on the billowy sea; human beings were in her, noble creatures, whose cry did knock against her very heart. Poor souls, they perished! Then saw she an old man and a maiden, admired Miranda, the top of admiration! and then a youth, one might call him a thing divine, for nothing natural one ever saw so noble! But look! a smile is on Ruth's lips (you cannot see her eyes, the lashes shade them so); a gentle, answering, kindling smile, for music is in the air. It is no mortal business or sound that the earth owes; the songster does his spiriting gently. Fine apparition! my quaint Ariel!

Perdita had awaked, and tried her customary arts to attract her mistress in vain. For a space she sat up erect, looking in her face with a suppressed mew; then rolled over and over on the gravel; then sprang on the stone, and rubbed against Ruth's foot, even reaching her hand, as it fell heedlessly by her side, until, finding herself utterly unheeded, she climbed the stone wall, whose irregular juttings gave her easy access to the top. There she stood, peeping now at Ruth, now over at the green lane on the other side, when a sudden cry startled the absorbed reader, and she looked up just in time to see a hand which had clutched the kitten suddenly withdrawn with its prize. Ruth flung down her Shakspeare, sprang from the tree to the wall, mounted rapidly to the top, and leaped into the lane below. There the figure of a retreating intruder stimulated her, and she ran rapidly on in pursuit. Once she had nearly gained him in the open lane, but he suddenly turned through some shrubbery adjoining. Ruth, still undaunted, kept on, gained another view of him, and at length saw him enter the Lyceum Hall, which had been newly erected in a retired part of the village. Had she paused for thought, her courage might have failed; but the only image in her mind was Perdita in that hateful air-pump, struggling for life. Pushing on, therefore, she threw open the door with all her force, and found herself in a hall of large dimensions, with a group of young men, one of whom was examining with great coolness the quiverings of a cat in' a receiver. Her alarm and modesty would unquestionably have overwhelmed her, had she not at the same moment seen a paw of Perdita peeping from out the waistcoat of the fugitive student. And who was that student? Willie White; his curls shorn, all but two that fell becomingly over his temples, while a long coat testified that he was looking up to the ranks of men. It is difficult to say which blushed the more deeply as their eyes met, while Mr. White, in endeavouring to screen Perdita from observation, gave her a squeeze that produced a melancholy and protracted mew. It was absolutely necessary for Ruth to say something, for her appearance and situation were becoming rather alarming. Her comb had fallen out in the chaise, leaving her long braided hair streaming down behind, and a rent was visible in her frock, which had caught in the bushes : still there was an elevated and wild grace in her air, which the toilet could not have given. She was about beginning with an apology for her appearance, but another mew from Perdita, and a suppressed smile among the young gentlemen, made her angry, and, going up to White, she said passionately,

"Give me my kitten this moment, sir. You have no right to it."

There was silence; the young gentlemen were too much ashamed to be just, and again they smiled, though in perplexity.

At this moment the first subject of their experiments gave her last convulsive and terrific gasp. Ruth started back in terror; then doubling her small hand, and almost stamping her foot in her excitement, while a bright red spot flushed in her cheek, she said, in a voice where sarcasm and indignation mingled,

"It is a pity that science should make thieves of gentlemen!"

Perhaps the taunt was displeasing to the young chemists, for they still seemed determined to carry off the thing cavalierly. Ruth's quick eye detected the expression of the group, and, feeling that her poor little pet was lost to her, she stood a moment silent, and then slowly turned to go away. She was too proud for tears, but there was a deep, unaffected expression of grief on her countenance that thrilled all their hearts, and the cry, "Give up the kitten, White! Let her have the kitten!" went round the hall. William, only too willing to perform this act of restitution, laid the panting little creature in Ruth's hands, whispering,

"Forgive me, Miss Raymond."

As she received the rescued victim, he met the reproachful glance of her now tearful eyes. Shaking her head impatiently, she deigned no answer, nor gave a look to the group behind; but, pressing Perdita close to her, ran as for life until she reached her home.

Willie White's dreams were perplexed that night by juvenile remembrances of the White Cat and the Beautiful Princess; and when he awoke it was to wonder if Ruth Raymond's smile was as lovely as her anger; while his companions long after remembered the flashing eye and lofty look of disdain with which she asked,

"Is science to make thieves of gentlemen?"

CHAPTER X.

Ruth's Bedroom.—Her Library.—Love Tokens.—Music.—Romances.—Ruth writes Poetry.

RUTH told over and over again to the various members of the family the tale of Perdita's rescue. Her
father looked grave, fearing that some feminine at-
tribute had been infringed upon ; her mother felt
somewhat triumphant ; the children quarrelled which
should have the honour of giving the kitten her supper,
and little Walter doubled up his fist as a challenge to
all future foes. Ruth retired to her apartment in unusual excitement. But let us look at that apartment ;
two years have passed since we were there in the reign
of *doll-ism.* The large closet, once the baby-house, is
now the *boudoir;* that is, Ruth calls it so when she
dates a letter to a young friend. Now was the reign
of girlhood : taste and judgment struggling with old
associations, an odd intermingling of the juvenile and
the mature. Pictures were Ruth's passion ; and, in
lieu of more valuable acquisitions, her wall was mostly
covered with daubs and caricatures, though it must be
confessed her eye rested with more complacency on
the divine expression of a Madonna, which was suspended, in strange juxtaposition, next to a stiff, flaunt-
ing costume of a fashion of three years standing on a
female, with a waist that nature never made. On her
dressing-table were accumulated the gifts of years, in
the shape of scent-bottles, and boxes of all forms and

hùes; while here and there might be seen a relic of the baby-house appropriated to useful or ornamental purposes. Her library bore the same marks of inequality. Berquin's Children's Friend, and even Barbauld's Lessons, which chanced to be well bound, looked out on the shelf beside Mrs. Chapone's Letters; a Goody Two-Shoes, to which some kindly private associations were attached, peeped out with its dog-cared leaves from behind Thomson's Seasons, while a Sunday-school Hymn-book, given her by her venerable pastor, was placed, with its defaced covers neatly pasted, beside a richly gilt Bible, the gift of her fourteenth birthday.

But the secular book most prized in her collection was a small volume then recently issued, an exquisite altar whereon the young imagination may kindle its early incense—Willis's Poems.

I aim at no criticism, no plummet and line for book-measuring here; but I ask any one just to place that volume in a young girl's hands, and see how the pulse of poetry will begin to throb, how her eyes will kindle and melt to tears, as some lofty or tender sentiment finds an echo in her bosom. In three months let him look at the book, and he will find it dark with pencil-lines, those little indexes of mind.

I have passed over several preferences with which various youths in round jackets had inspired Ruth, as too ephemeral to register; but there were indications of these things all around her; initials in pencil, on her panels and books, and initials written with diamond on the window-pane, ineffaceable, alas! too, for the individual was forgotten; here was a faded flower carefully folded up; there was a picture or toy without any attraction but from its association with the giver;

on a piece of paper which the housemaid swept out,
was written,

"I shall *never* forget Saturday night, June 18th.
Blissful ! blissful !"

A sprig of arbor vitæ shared the same fate ; it went
down to the dust unhonoured, with these words attached to it:

"Presented me, February 9th, by J. C. Long as
memory retains its empire shall I remember the evening."

Then on books and slips of paper might be seen stale
poetical passages with marked italics.

> "Where'er I go, whatever realms I see,
> My HEART untravell'd fondly turns to *thee.*
> The course of *true* love never did run smooth," &c., &c.

In the retirement of this familiar room, alone and
undisturbed, Ruth's voice began to swell rich and full
with her guitar accompaniment ; and as she tested the
power of her own tones, Orphéan fables seemed real-
ized to her imagination ; the summits of the hills
around her stood out in clearer lines, the clouds group-
ed up in more pillowy masses, and the trees waved in
more graceful play. It was here too that romance
threw its mysterious foldings around her, shutting out
the world, and making the page on which she dwelt the
theatre of passion. Here, kindled to an indignation
beyond control, she dashed the unoffending volume of
the Children of the Abbey on the floor, when Amanda
was caught in the snares of a villain ; here she sobbed
herself into a headache over the fate of Paul and Virginia ; here she shook with terror at the wild horrors
of Maturin ; here she glowed and trembled with Jean-
nie Deans ; gasped for breath as the trapdoor fell

over the lovely and unconscious Amy Robsart, and
turned from the chimney-corner lest she should see
Lucy Ashton making mouths and chattering in its recess.   And it was here that Ruth first surprised herself
with her own rhymes.   Was it possible, she asked herself, that she had written *three* whole verses ?   How
delicious was the title !

" To the first Violet."

She trod the room elastically ; it seemed like a
dream, yet there it was, " flower and bower," " leaf and
brief," " see and tree," palpable to her eye, full of eu-
phony to her ear ; and those thoughts, were they born
of her, that exquisite image of *the violet shrinking like
a modest maiden ?*

Ruth copied it in her best hand, went to the door,
turned back, and then, gathering resolution, carried it,
conscious and blushing, to her mother.   Mrs. Raymond was delighted, and, encouraged by her mother's
praise, she went to her father, who was reading a review on the literature of Modern Europe.   At first
her eyes were cast down, then raised in intense and
painful interest as his moved from line to line.   He
returned her the paper with the least possible shrug
of his shoulders, and something of a smile, it might be
of approbation, but it looked a little quizzical as he
said,

" The first piece, you say, my dear ; take care of
sing-song.   Moderate prose is always better than moderate poetry."

Ruth walked quietly and somewhat slowly out of the
apartment, and shut *that* door softly ; but the next and
the next were slammed to with increasing vehemence
until she reached her own, which she double-locked.

Then came the whirlwind of a first literary mortification.   She stamped up and down the apartment, tore
" The first Violet" to fragments, and threw herself on
the bed in almost hysterical agony.

CHAPTER XI.

The Age of Presumption.—Despondency.—Religious Love.

THE impetuosity and decision of character which was so interesting in its occasional developments, began to make Ruth less attractive in her domestic relations. Feeling her power in some things, she claimed the right of judgment in all. And this is the period when it is most difficult to preserve perfect sympathy between parent and child; the former forgets too often that infancy has gone, and that Providence itself has given that self-will to youth, whose very mistakes teach the most profound lessons; while the child, feeling no longer the want of leading-strings, throws them off impatiently, seeking no substitute in paternal love for paternal care. The age of fifteen is the age of presumption; but it is one of deep and impassioned feeling, of wild transitions, self-abasement, triumph. Few reflect upon the trials of this chrysalis state, when the butterfly spirit of youth throbs and beats against the prison-shell of childhood. At this age of incipient power there is frequently deep despondency. Often when her will was thwarted, and sometimes when it was not, this distrust fell upon Ruth. Her parents seemed tyrannical, her friends to have forsaken her, and she wept in secret with a bitterness that should only belong to sin and experience. These things are necessary to the dark and narrow path by which man enters on the table-land of faith and *love;* and thus

Ruth, surrounded by friends, flushed with health, felt often unloved and lonely; and when a common eye saw no grief-cloud on her horizon, breathed a despairing wish that the grave might cover her.

Ruth rose one morning in this state of nervous excitement; she was disrespectful or cold to her parents, tyrannical to the children, and dictatorial to the servants, bearing about with her the air of one who had been aggrieved, without asking sympathy. She struggled against her feelings, knowing that her smiles made sunshine in her home; that they were reflected on her father's brow, and settled in her mother's heart. She busied herself in her studies, and tried to beguile herself with amusements, but all seemed stale and unprofitable. The day passed away, and she sat alone (for her unsocial mood had driven all away) on the door-sill, where a few years before she had watched the dissolving icicle. It was an autumnal twilight; the evening gust brought leaf after leaf in faded yellow to her feet, and drove the flitting clouds rapidly by. As the darkness gathered, a sound of music was borne on the air; that sound the most mirthful when the heart is gay, the saddest when it is sorrowful; the preceding strain of a violin for the dance. Ruth listened, and slow tears dropped like that once dissolving icicle from her eyes. She was utterly forsaken and forlorn. By-and-by a star or two smiled out through the scudding clouds, and then the moon followed, tinging those clouds with glory. A sudden flash, I know not what, as if from the spear of Ithuriel, came on Ruth's mind, enlightening and subduing, and a voice seemed to say, " God made thee, and he loves thee." Her tears were checked; the thought of Deity overshadowed her; the firmament shrank away ; star after star shrank in the distance, and prayer was on her lips. She rose softly, went to her bedroom, and would have kneeled by her bedside, but the privacy there was not deep enough ; groping her way to a recess behind the chimney, form-ed by a sloping roof, she threw herself on her knees. *It was the first prayer of her soul.* Sorrow for sin, hope of pardon, struggled on her eloquent lips ; the fountains of religious faith were unsealed and gushed forth, and rested not until the spirit of *love* descended on her with a seal of peace. Ruth returned to the family. A sweet repose was in her manner, though her eyes bore traces of tears. Her father wondered at the new tenderness of her air, but her mother guessed that she had been with God.

CHAPTER XII.

Ruth Sixteen.—Her Apartment.—Seals.—Ruth Romantic.—Her
Mortification.—Development of Mind.—Invitation to a Ball.

THE reign of girlhood is over, and Ruth, in brilliant,
sensitive sixteen, sits by her toilet, contemplating the
changes which her mother's thoughtful affection has
made in her apartment; the new flowing curtains, the
well-matched furniture, and the large mirror substituted
for the small one, in which she could discern only a
modicum of her pretty person! Ruth rose and walked
towards it, then backward; the image there was certainly lovely, and it smiled as it saw that even its feet were
visible. As she stood thus, lost in admiration partly of
herself and partly of her acquisition, she perceived
some one in the glass mimicking her tiptoe movement
and making grimaces; it was her brother Frederic.
Ruth blushed, slapped him, half in anger, and locked
the door.

Do you ask how Ruth looked? Think of your love-
liest friend, and you may partially behold her; for every
one said, when talking with Ruth five minutes, "How
much Miss Raymond reminds me of some one!" She
gave another glance at herself, sat down to her centre-
table, and looked around once more to see if aught yet
could be done to perfect her arrangement. No picture
remained conspicuous but the Madonna; and Ruth
seemed now, from her mother's care, to understand better than ever the soft loving eye whose fringed lids were
bent on her child. She passed a short time over her

work-box, arranging its little elegances, and then, as if a sudden thought moved her, opened her writing-desk and took out her seals. They were just now her passion; the little horde had increased until she had graduated every sentiment from the most bald ceremony to the most tender regard. She threw aside one which bore the scriptural and to me delightful name of *Ruth* (alas, the owner was ashamed of her oldfashioned patronymic!), and selecting *Pour toujours*, began the following note.

"DEAR ISABEL,

"It is an age since I have seen you. Have you forgotten our walk by the bridge? 'Have all your oaths and protestations come to this?' Meet me under the willow at sunset, and love still your

"RUTHIANA."

An interruption prevented Ruth from sealing her note, and a gust of wind carried it into the entry. Ruth searched for it in vain; and the next morning, Frederic, who, like some other brothers in the world, seemed to think a sister's feelings but a toy to play with, read it aloud with much gravity, laying a painful stress on the signature.

The shout that followed was overwhelming; even Mr. Raymond was inexpressibly diverted, and gave vent to a cachinnation that rang on Ruth's ear with metallic harshness. She bent over her coffee with blushes; and from that day, when she betrayed any affectation, for Ruth did occasionally show symptoms of that disease, the nickname of Ruthiana was buzzed

F

about the little circle.   Thus salutary, though painful, are the unfoldings of domestic intercourse.

But Ruth, with all her foibles, had an abundant reserve of sound and valuable good sense.   Having passed the drill of elementary teaching, she began to apply her resources and educate herself.   She did not, like some girls, rush to romances as a novelty, for her parents had allowed her for several years to read one alternately with a solid book ; thus the great mass of her thoughts were on the latter, which lay long in her hands, while the novels were hurried through for the narrative.   It was delightful now to see the use Ruth made of her new liberty.   Romance and history were read to illustrate each other, and those works of fancy only selected where authorship claimed literary respect. ´ Her room began to assume the air of a study, though brightened and polished, of course, by feminine taste.

But much was Ruth upset in her grave pursuits one day, when a card for her first ball was placed in her hands.   Down went her maps, over fell a globe, and as she descended two stairs at a time to show it to her mother, MISS RAYMOND never appeared to her to have stood in such conspicuous letters.   An immediate consultation was held.

" Everybody has a *new* dress for the first ball, mamma," said Ruth ; " *every*body."

" What, if they have a frock they have worn only twice ?" said Mrs. Raymond, smiling.

The white muslin was brought from the drawer, and, after much searching, Ruth certainly detected a small spot on the front breadth ; and the decision was, that Ruth should have a new muslin dress, with a pale pink flower in her hair, and Isabel was to be asked to wear the same.

Ruth was restless that night, and dreamed that, as she was beginning to *balance* to William White at the ball, Perdita peeped out from his waistcoat and mewed.

CHAPTER XIII.

A Funeral Bell.—The Village Burial.—Ruth and a Stranger.

THERE was something touching and solemn in the obsolete custom of a funeral bell. I have felt its influence in town and country. In a city it recalled me from the rush and hurry of life to muse and think of death.   I did not ask the village question, Who is dead? but the very thought that none of the passers-by knew who had gone to his last account, made human weakness show still more frail.   In the country, that sound accorded well with the voice of nature ; swelling to the hills, echoed in the valleys, it told its warning tale with tenderer emphasis.

An old schoolmistress of the village died, and Ruth, with her mother, went to pay the accustomed respect to her remains.   They walked contemplatively along, musing or moralizing in serious harmony with the tolling bell, until they reached the mansion of the deceased among the first visiters.   Her family sat around in quiet sorrow, while ranged in the entry, in a simple uniform of white, with black ribands, stood her pupils. For a time deep silence dwelt in the apartment of the women; then a low hum, as sympathy or curiosity found utterance.   As each new-comer entered, the mourners looked down more steadfastly, and the uninterested glanced up furtively in silence ; then the whispers became more assured, and worldly subjects entered in, in tones modulated and lengthened by the lugubrious associations of death.   Now the voices from without were gradually heard, rising from the suppressed tone of sympathy to social greeting, and once a laugh grated strangely on Ruth's nerves. She had never attended a funeral, and her heart beat fast as she saw the long, fresh-looking coffin, with its plated ornaments, and faster still when, following her mother, she looked in, and dwelt on the face of the dead, the pinched and colourless features, the sunken eyes, the thin gray hairs smoothed on the skinny brow, and the cold blue lips. Ruth remembered that those lips had taught her the rudiments of knowledge, and she sat down in tears.

The coffin-lid was screwed down; and as the venerable clergyman, in trembling tones, prayed that *her* death, who had gone to heaven's portal just before *his* turn had come, might be sanctified to the young, whom she had taught good knowledge, and to the aged, who had walked thus far with her through this vale of tears, stifled sobs were heard around. The coffin was borne out; the little girls, wiping their eyes, followed, preceding the relatives and near friends, who were called by name, down the lane. The remaining visiters were next invited to walk; and as they reached the door, the nearest gentleman silently tendered his arm to the lady that came in turn. Ruth, agitated and blinded by sympathetic tears, with downcast eyes, passively took an offered arm. The burial-place was half a mile distant. Ruth's companion was silent, and she could not utter a syllable, though the couple before them talked unrestrainedly. Pausing at a winding road along the base of a hill, the procession assumed an air of romantic interest apart from its solemnity, the white-robed girls standing in contrast with the sable-clothed mourners. Ruth's companion looked on them with rapt at-

F 2

tention.   " There is something very touching," said the
young man (Ruth had an instinct that he was young),
" there is something very touching in the spectacle
of these innocent children following to the grave one
so old."

" Yes, sir," said Ruth, falteringly.

There was a pause.

" Nature has blessed this spot with peculiar beauty,"
said the young gentleman (for Ruth was sure that
he was a young *gentleman*) ; " one might be willing to
die *here*."

Another pause.

" Were you acquainted with this old lady ?" asked
the young man.

Ruth's heart-strings began to loosen at this question ; self was forgotten, and her childlike spirit re-
vived.

She told about her early school-days ; how, even then,
though it was so long ago, Mrs. Ramsay was very aged,
and how nicely she used to look in her armchair on
the sanded floor, with her mob cap and folded kerchief;
and how sorry she was she had ever been roguish and
offended her; and how she knew she must be happy, because she was so good, and how lonely the house would
look when old Mrs. Ramsay no longer sat by the door
in summer under the honeysuckle arbour, and how she
should miss her in the next pew at church, where she
had handed her over the hymn-book, with the psalms
open, for ten years.

Ruth was somewhat astonished when they reached
the graveyard, and her grief was renewed as the little
girls parted on the right and left at the gate, and the
procession passed through to the open grave.   Then

the gentlemen fell back to allow the children and the women to advance, and Ruth lost her companion.

The children and mourners circled round the grave and wept. But why? Who should mourn when the ripened shock falls to the ground? No smiling babe, torn from its mother's bosom, closed there its innocent eyes; no youth, in the flush and glow of existence, treading on life's flowers ; no citizen, faithfully working out his duties, and struggling with its cares. She who had gone had budded, bloomed, ripened, and decayed; her task was done, the servant was called to her wages, the heir to the supper of love.

On returning from the funeral, Ruth was eloquent in praise of her late companion.

" I will venture anything, mamma," said she, " that he is the Alfred Clarendon who is one of the junior managers of the ball."

" Why so ?" said her mother.

"He *looks* as if he were," answered Ruth, " or, rather, he *speaks* as if he were, for my eyes were so red I was ashamed to look up at him fully."

After walking on in silence for some time, Ruth said, with the faintest possible tinge of consciousness in her manner,

" Do you not think, mamma, that there was something very touching in the aspect of those children following one so old to the funeral ?"

She had appropriated nearly every word of her partner.

CHAPTER XIV.

Ruth's Sabbath and Church.

RUTH rose on the Sabbath following, and hushed earth's cares to rest as they fluttered in her bosom.

Beautiful Sabbath, soft halcyon on life's turbid waters! how blessingly dost thou come to the weary, how brightly to the gay! What blue depths thy stillness lends to the heavens, speaking of infinity : what reposing verdure to the earth, telling of love. Even over the city's cramped habitations, the Sabbath morning clouds fold their white wings and rest, as if waiting for the prayers of thousands to lift them up, or float gently away to yield the upward eye a glimpse of heaven. Beautiful Sabbath, soft halcyon in life's turbid waters, *I* bless thee!

And Ruth blessed the Sabbath. It was to her a day of *love*. Restrained, but not depressed, her thoughts turned inward, while her little bark of life lay still in its tranquil harbour.

She turned from her morning toilet to the window, where a fall of snow in the night had wrought its fairy changes; the lingering leaves of autumn contrasted glowingly with the sunlit frostwork below and around, and as they dropped in the stillness one by one, with golden and crimson dies, it seemed as if nature, like some tired beauty, threw listlessly off the drapery of her triumphant hours.

Chilled with the frosty air, Ruth threw her fur cape

about her, and traversing her apartment, committed to memory the hundred and third psalm. Its tenderness accorded well with her gentle spirit; and as the kindling verses at the close flowed on like a trumpet-tone, her heart expanded, and she cried aloud with clasped hands and uplifted eyes, " Bless the Lord, oh *my* soul !"

But Ruth was mortal, and when the bell rang for church her straw bonnet was tied on with a consciousness of becomingness; and, even when her foot was on the threshold, she ran back to a glass to adjust a blue riband that contrasted with her throat, like one of her own violets on a snowbank, until the voice of her mother chiding her delay, brought her back to religious duty.

When were we at church before with Ruth? Not since her baptism, when her eyes were closed in feebleness, her heart still as the valley flower where winds come not ; when tiptoe youth stood gazing at the little stranger, and old age knew not whether to feel joy or sorrow that a child was born into the world.

Ruth's second visit to church was at the age of three years. Clasping her mother's hand, she toiled or leaped up the ascent, pausing here and there to gather a flower or pick up a pebble, prattling of infantine nothings until entering the porch. Then, with her little features composed to a pleasant demureness, she was lifted to a three-cornered seat opposite her mother, where she thrust out her new morocco shoes for the benefit of spectators, or knocked them against the bench to their annoyance. The first expedient resorted to by Mrs. Raymond to divert her restlessness, was to give her a *bouquet* of flowers at the commencement of the sermon, with permission to pull them to pieces.

Ruth was very earnest in this procedure for several Sundays; and as she arose at " amens," threw a shower of blossoms from her lap that almost made her a personification of Thomson's Spring.

It so chanced that one morning a farmer sat *dos-d-dos* to Ruth in the next pew, who bore about with him one of the last queues of this generation. Overcome by his entire cessation from physical effort, he fell asleep, and Mrs. Raymond, having provided Ruth with a lap full of flowers, became absorbed in the sermon. The pressure of the top of the pew brought the farmer's queue to a horizontal position with Ruth's ear. She pushed it gently aside several times, and scratched the tickled extremity; but, finding the annoyance continue, turned her head round and faced it. It was so closely wound about with black riband from the roots of the hair to the end where it was fastened with a bow, that its whole length, which was about a quarter of a yard, stood out as compact and stiff as a pipestem, except at the end, which dwindled off to the quantity of a hair-pencil. Ruth eyed it at first with a simple, serious kind of curiosity, as it moved in regular play with the somewhat laboured breathing of the sleeper; at length she ventured just to touch it with her forefinger. At that moment the farmer, who dreamed that a thunder-gust was rising over his hay-field, gave a perceptible start, and the queue looked so living with its sympathetic jerk, that Ruth withdrew her hand and resumed her childish stare. As the dreamer's thunder-squall passed over, the queue and Ruth became more composed. She raised her finger again, touched it timidly, and, finding it harmless, ventured to play with its brush-like end; then, with great gravity of countenance and quietness of manner, took a full-blown tulip from her lap, and thrust the stem through the black bow.

Mrs. Raymond was interrupted in a most edifying induction of the preacher by an irresistible laugh in the adjoining pew, where some children had been beguiling their own weariness by looking at Ruth's experiments. She followed their eyes to the child, who sat innocently watching the pendulum movements of the ornamented queue.

Mrs. Raymond's situation was inexpressibly awkward. To tell Ruth to remove the tulip, or arise to do it herself, was equally embarrassing. In vain did she shake her head and lift her warning finger; Ruth was too much absorbed to notice her, and proceeded to add a lily of the valley to this novel flower-vase. As Mrs. Raymond's feelings were raised to actual agony, little Ruth fortunately looked at her, and, perceiving her mother's glance of despair, and thinking she wished for the flowers, removed them with a twitch that fairly awoke the sleeper, and handed them to her with a silent smile.

When Ruth began to write, and became the happy owner of a silver pencil, her hymn-book bore ample testimony to her industry. When forbidden to draw cats and faces, and particularly the farmer's queue, she began systematically to darken the centre of every letter O; then, as her ideas expanded, she marked and marked again her favourite hymns and verses. By-and-by she began to commit them to memory; then her voice was heard mingling faintly yet sweetly with the choir; then passages in the Bible arrested her attention; then the text was remembered; then a glance at her mother told that some appeal in the sermon was understood and felt; and last, prayer brooded over her with holy wings. Thus, from Sabbath to Sabbath, were golden trains laid for memory and hope; mines which were to be worked by the undying spirit through all eternity.

But Ruth is sixteen, and is no longer *led* up that church-crowned hill. Supporting her mother's enfeebled footsteps, she enters reverentially the sacred walls, and treads the accustomed aisle.

Various are the modes of entering church. There is the don't-care manner, and an easy, home-like step, which says all places are alike to me; there is the conscious manner, which betrays that one is thinking of human eyes instead of that which searches hearts; there is the worldly manner, with the out-of-door jest or speculation lingering around the lips; there is the affected manner, lolling this side and that, or mincing with the feet; there is the bravado manner, a holding up of the head, and a swinging of the arms, with long strides; there is the new-dress manner, with all sorts of consciousness; there is the mourning manner, with the eyes and heart cast down, God only knows with what degree of suffering; there is the bride manner, where bashfulness and pride alternately prevail; there is the rapid or high-pressure manner, which dashes on with the sole object of being seated; there is the side-long manner, where a glance is thrown and withdrawn on the instant; there is the inquisitive manner, with the look up and about to know who is there; there is the languid manner, which determines not to be in a hurry, even if the service has begun; there is the supercilious manner, which says, stand off, I am (not holier, but) more fashionable or wealthy than thou; there is the gracious manner (sometimes political), which wishes to be agreeable to everybody; there is the shuffling manner, which pitches itself into a pew as it can; there is the fidgeting manner, which cannot get easily seated; there is the stranger manner, which looks about anxiously, and seems rescued when it attains accommodation; there is the decrepit manner, thinking only of its own infirmities; there is the awkward manner, which stumbles in the aisle, goes to the wrong pew, and fumbles at the button on the door.

Ruth's, my own Ruth's, was the serenely *reverential* manner. The church was holy ground to her: no worldly whispering desecrated its solemn hour. That hour was strictly God's; there was enough beside for the world, that was for Him. If she pleaded for mercy, or rejoiced in hope in prayer, no one knew, for her face was shaded from intrusive eyes; if her golden notes mingled with the choir, she cared not who heard but Heaven; and when the pastor unfolded the will of God, she laid it meekly to her own heart and was still.

Ruth loved her pastor; he had touched her forehead with the baptismal element; his explanatory words and kindly smile had enlightened her Sunday lessons; and, now that her mind was capable of reasoning, she listened in public with attention, and communicated privately her ignorance and doubts to the good old man, who, though standing on the confines of another world, was not chilled to this.

Happy Ruth, to *love* your pastor; to be able to look up, from year to year, to eyes that beam kindly on you; to hear heavenly truths from lips endeared by sympathy; to feel almost a partner in the eloquence that thrills the hearts around you; to be taught immortality, the *life for ever*, by one with whom you could wish to live eternally.

G

CHAPTER XV.

Dresses of Heroines in Novels.—Heroines of Poetry.—Ruth and her Mantuamaker.—Progress of Mind.—Ruth at the Ball.—New Acquaintance.—An Accident.

PATTERNS of white muslin for Ruth's dress went to and fro with as anxious an investigation as if the company at the ball were to spy her with microscopes ; and the decision being made, Miss Homefield, the best mantuamaker in the village, was rescued from among a crowd of applicants to cut for the important occasion.

Novelists have taken great pride in the wardrobe of their heroines. The hand that Sir Charles Grandison bowed over rested on the richest brocade ; the Evelinas and Cecilias were patterns of good taste ; and Miss Owenson's Glorvina sported a gauze dress of " woven air ;" but who remembers these things ?

Poets, on the contrary, avoiding this minuteness of description, have, by a few strong and simple intellectual touches, conveyed the image of their thoughts to ours with a fidelity that stamps them at once on our memories ; so strongly, indeed, that no friend is more near than these creatures of the imagination. . Who cannot see among a thousand,

" The tender blue" of Medora's " large, loving eye ?"

Gulnare too,

" That form with eye so dark and cheek so fair,
  And auburn waves of gemm'd and braided hair,
  With shape of fairy likeness—naked foot,
  That shines like snow, and falls on earth as mute."

All the costumes of the novelist would not bring Gertrude, as Campbell has done, before us in her loveliness, nor show

> "Those eyes affectionate and glad,
> That seem'd to love whate'er they look'd upon ;
> Whether with Hebe's mirth her features shone,
> Or if a shade more pleasing them o'ercast,
> As if for heavenly musing meant alone ;
> Yet so becomingly the expression pass'd
> That each succeeding look was lovelier than the last."

Scott, almost as an exception, has entered into detail in the dress of the heroines of his poetry ; he had a geographical mind, and loved to locate them ; Ellen, for instance :

> "A chieftain's daughter seem'd the maid ;
> Her *satin snood*, her *silken plaid*,
> Her *golden brooch* such birth betray'd ;
> And seldom was a snood amid
> Such wild, luxuriant ringlets hid,
> Whose glossy black to shame might bring
> The plumage of the raven's wing.
> And seldom ever breast so fair
> Mantled a plaid with modest care,
> And never brooch the folds combined,
> Above a heart more good and kind."

Yet, after the snood, and brooch, and plaid are forgotten, we " gaze on Ellen's eye."

Wordsworth is singularly happy in making his pictures stand out on his poetical canvass. Take any age.

The girl of fourteen.

> " Sweet Highland girl, a very shower
> Of beauty is thy earthly dower !
> A face with gladness overspread !
> Sweet looks by human kindness bred,
> And seemliness complete, that sways
> Thy courtesies, about thee plays."

A maiden.

"A dancing shape, an image gay,
    To haunt, to startle and way-lay."

Childhood.

"Her eyes were fair and very fair,
    Her beauty made me glad."

Early Infancy.

            "On thy face
Smiles are beginning like the beams of dawn
To shoot and circulate—
Feelers of love."

A matron.

"She was a woman of a steady mind,
    Tender and deep in her excess of love;
    Not speaking much, pleased rather with the joy
    Of her own thoughts."

Another.

        "Graceful was her port;
A lofty stature, undepress'd by time,
Whose visitation had not spared to touch
The finer lineaments of frame and face,
To that complexion brought which prudence trusts in,
And wisdom loves."

Milton felt no want of a wardrobe for his "accomplished Eve;" and, though Spenser clothes his delicate Una, in the Faery Queene, it is with such rare simplicity as to throw back our thoughts on her intellectual purity.   At first we see her

"Under a vele that wimpled was full low,
    And over all a black stole did shee throw."

Then

"In secret shadow, far from all men's sight,
    From her fayre head her fillet she undight,
    And lay'd her stole aside.   Her angel face
    As the great eye of heaven shyned bright,
    And made a sunshine in the shady place."

Then,

> " Fair and fresh as freshest flower in May,
> And on her now a garment did she weare,
> All lily-white, withouten spot or pride."

Perhaps the best, though an unconscious satire on over-dressing a heroine, may be found in the description of a ballroom attire in a novel entitled " A Summer at Weymouth."

" Sir Edward sent to let the ladies know that he was in the drawing-room, and hoped they were ready ; and the business of the toilet being completed, they descended immediately. Mrs. Moreland led the countess to the admiral, who was in his naval uniform, with a superb diamond star, being a Knight of the Bath ; he saluted his niece, and admired the *delicate taste* displayed in her dress, which was white thin satin, covered with British lace, the train and drapery of the same, made with beautiful borders expressly for the purpose ; wreathed with *hawthorn* blossoms, and looped up with braids of *riband-grass,* which also formed knots, confining small bouquets of *violets, primroses, lilies of the valley,* and *wild roses ;* full lace sleeves were drawn up with small wreaths of *riband-grass* and *violets,* over armlets of *rubies* and *emeralds,* forming a chain, each link fastened with a single *brilliant ;* a corresponding chain formed the cestus, and ornamented the dress beneath a full tucker of lace, which, with her lappets, was also made in Great Britain ; her hair, in tasteful *puffs* and *ringlets,* was encircled by a wreath of *jessamine,* in *brilliants* and *emeralds,* tied on the left side with a knot of *brilliants,* which confined three *white feathers ;* necklace, earrings, and shoe-bows of *diamonds,* com-

pleted her dress, which was *neat, elegant,* and becoming."

But all this time Ruth is standing before her mantuamaker, with the folds of her white muslin flowing
about her youthful form.   What different associations
are called up by that simple manufacture?   It is the
first ornamental dress of girls; it is gathered around
the widow's face, shading her sorrowing eyes; and it
lies on the cold corpse, covering the altered lip and
brow, while the hand that slowly raises it starts as its
moving folds give seeming motion to the dead.

But Ruth moralized not on white muslin.

"What is the last fashion for dresses, Miss Homefield?" said she to the demure-looking personage before her.

"We does not be governed by any particular fashion," replied Miss Homefield, with a subdued air.
"We studies the expression.   There is a great deal,
Miss Raymond," she continued, with solemnity, clip-
ping with the scissors so closely to Ruth's neck that she
winced, "there is a great deal in adopting the cut to
the figur.   Yours, I should say," and she glanced on
Ruth's mantling cheek, "is elegant bloom."

Ruth looked meekly at the careering scissors, and
then triumphantly at her mirror.

"You seem to have quite a considerable collection
of books," said Miss Homefield, just darting up her
eyes, without pausing in her occupation.   Have you
read (a little to the right, if you please) a work that's
out about the Missouri lands?   Now it's *my* notion (a
pin, I thank you) that the lands should be drained (this
is the Grecian fold, miss) before they are dressed.
Books, Miss Raymond (we will put this fold a little
lower on the bust), is great enlighteners."

Much to Ruth's surprise, her frock sat exquisitely, and the expression designed to be *elegant bloom* satisfied her highly. The pure white of the muslin certainly contrasted well with her glowing cheeks and lustrous eyes. A girl never looks prettier than with a mantuamaker, sideling and glancing, advancing and retreating, half in jest, half in earnest, conscious of newness without the temptation to display.

The long-expected evening came, and Ruth, committed to the especial care of Dr. Gesner, on account of the indisposition of her mother, joined Isabel and her parents. Oh that long interval after dressing, waiting the silly call of fashion, when playfulness is exhausted, when the hour for rest comes on without repose, and even hope is tired of hoping! Ruth and Isabel fairly yawned in each other's faces, until the carriage wheels roused them, and they sprang up like awakened statues.

Ruth kissed her father with tenderness, and lingered for a moment to catch her mother's smile, for well she knew their thoughts would follow her: and she sighed as she returned once more to press her mother's cheek, that it looked so pale, and that the parental eye could not watch her still.

The resources of the village had been exhausted to meet this yearly ball; and the managers, finding the tavern hall too small for their purpose, had arranged a vacant barn for the reception of their guests. The flooring was planed and chalked, the walls hung with evergreens from the woods, flowers from greenhouses, and variegated lamps from the city. An illuminated arch at the entrance dazzled Ruth by its unexpected brilliancy, and prevented her noticing the manager, who advanced, and, detaching her from Dr. Gesner, offered her his arm and conducted her across the building.

" Beautiful, beautiful," exclaimed Ruth, in the admiration of the moment, as the tasteful and brilliant arrangement burst upon her. ." Who did it all ?"

" The managers must divide the credit," said her conductor.

Ruth started, and looked up quickly.   Their eyes met with a sudden, delicious understanding, and she blushed so deeply, that Miss Homefield's intended expression of " elegant bloom" was lost; she ought to have been dressed like a milkmaid.

" You walked with me to the funeral," said Ruth with her characteristic quickness, as the blush passed away.   " How strange !"

". You walked with me to the funeral," said the young man.   " How delightful !"

" I just wish to guess *one* thing," said Ruth, with irrepressible earnestness ; " are you not Alfred Clarendon ?" .

" I am," said the gentleman, smiling.   " Will Miss Raymond allow me the pleasure of dancing with her in the first set ?"

Ruth acquiesced, and he left her for his duties as manager.

" I told mamma so," she said, almost clapping her hands as she turned to Isabel; " I told mamma his name was Clarendon !"

The set was called.   Ruth had practised a good deal for this ball, and her mirror had seen some antics she would not have betrayed to other spectators.   She meant to *balancer* this way, and *dos-à-dos* that way, and hold her arms so, and her head so ; but the

first burst of the band dispersed all affectation. She
gave herself up to the impulses of the moment, to the
fascination of sight and sound ; and the joy would have
been almost frolic had it not been restrained by natural dignity. There was none of the fastidiousness of
fashion about her ; whatever seemed to be worth en-
joying, she enjoyed ; and, like an unforced plant, turned her branches to the sunshine.

Ruth was introduced in form to William White.
She threw herself back daintily, and he bowed frigid-
ly, and they stood opposite each other in the cotillon
with a grave and conscious air, until, as Ruth turned
him in the dance, a sudden impulse came over her, and
in a low but distinct tone, with her eyes raised roguishly and then cast down, she said " mew !"

The effect was irresistible ; not to laugh was to die
of convulsions ; the barrier of reserve was thrown
down, and they were no longer strangers. This is the
peculiar charm of frankness, when modified by pure
and chaste manners, that it calls mind in contact with
mind, and does the work of years ; but what Ruth
gained with William White she lost with the two Miss
Longworths in pink satin, who asserted the next day
that Miss Raymond ridiculed them *publicly*.

Clarendon again sought Ruth's hand in the dance.
He trod the measure gracefully enough, but it was in
his moments of repose that he was the favourite partner ; here Ruth, as he led the way, found herself on
higher ground than she had ever attained before. Efforts at reasoning, unstudied criticism, and the kinder
lore of the affections, fell from her unconsciously ; yet
demands from another quarter on her good-nature were
equally successful, and she often stopped good Dr. Ges-

ner in a yawn like the opening of a crater as he stood near, until he roused himself, and watched her motions as he would those of a grasshopper, calling her his papilio, a favourite epithet since their race by the riv-er-side.

And now the social hilarity of the scene reached its height in a Pendleton reel, when, as the band poured forth its fullest tones, and almost the whole company were in motion, glancing like winged birds from side to side, a crash was heard; the foundation gave way, the floor sank, and the dancers after it. There went the Miss Longworths' pink satins, Miss Kidman's five ostrich feathers, Miss Halway's bird of paradise plume, Miss Able's blond cape, and Miss Notable's imi-tation; and Ruth went too, bursting off in her descent the hooks and eyes from Miss Homefield's "elegant bloom expression." The first consciousness that she possessed was that she was sitting on a soft but firm substance, and a guttural sound announed to her that she was making an unintentional divan of Dr. Ges-ner's body.

"Oh, dear Dr. Gesner, is it you?" said Ruth, pa-thetically.

"Ees, my papilio. Sit easy, if you please, and ask one gentleman, for the loves of Heaven, to take himself off of my *leichdorn*, what you call corn on se toe."

The various involuntary actors in this scene rose slowly, their gallant array sadly broken. Ruth un-hitched a bunch of Miss Longworth's false curls from Dr. Gesner's button, and brushed his soiled coat with her handkerchief, while he gradually recovered his short and husky breathing. As she stood thus forget-ting herself in bringing him to good-humour, Clarendon passed, and hurriedly asked leave to inquire after her health to-morrow; while William White, with jest and laughter, escorted her home.

When Ruth reached the door of her home, she check-ed the laugh upon her lips, and entered with tiptoe steps, fearing to disturb the repose of her parents; but their vigilant thoughts were upon her, and the call of " Ruth, Ruth," as she passed their door, purposely left open, arrested her. Her father met her with a kind smile and a surprised look at her brilliant disarray. Entering her mother's apartment, she sat by the bed-side, and, throwing her arms about her, told them the joys and mishaps of the evening. Nothing is lovelier than the sweet temper of a weary girl, who, after an entertainment, or, perchance, disappointment, is over, returns and throws the light of good-humour on her home; the triumphs of beauty or of genius fade away before this charm; but when they are all united, the parent may well gaze with the subdued worship of a loving heart on his child. And Ruth was indeed love-lier as she poured out her feelings, her mother's hand in hers, her red cheek resting on her mother's pillow, than when sparkling and graceful she glided amid the dance. Their blessing followed her to her apartment. And there Ruth composed her busy thoughts to life's more holy aims. She had never yet neglected to offer her nightly prayers, and now they seemed to bear her fluttered spirit to sleep with a blessing.

C 2

CHAPTER XVI.

The Morning Slumberer.—The Cape Ann Housemaid.—The Morn-
ing-call.—Sunday-school Project.—The Farmer and his Wife.—
The Intemperate.—The Poor and Suffering.

THE morning sun shone brightly, but unheeded,
through Ruth's curtains; her young sister caressed
her with her usual endearments, but the twining arm
and playful kiss were unfelt; her brothers rushed to
the door, shouting, " Ruth, sister Ruth, wake up and
tell us about the ball ;" but she slept on; her mother
came with her soft tread and looked in upon her.
The girl's breathing was so tranquil, her look of repose so deep, such an utter absence of life's cares
dwelt on her, that she had not the heart to wake her;
so, just touching her roselike cheek with her lips, and
smoothing away the dishevelled hair from her neck,
she sighed softly, whispered " sleep on, poor child," and
descended to the breakfast-room. An hour passed
away, and Bridget the housemaid was sent to rouse
the slumberer.

" You're a pretty one, Miss Ruth," said Bridget, as
she went *clumping* into the room with her leather shoes,
and laid her rough hand on Ruth's shoulder, " to be
knocked up by one night's Jigging. I reckon you'd
be up to a thing or two more if you'd been bred down
at Cape Ann. The gals there used to dance the double shuffle till two in the mornin, and at sunrise were
singin over their brooms and washtubs like thrushes.
I was the gal, Miss Ruth," continued Bridget, with in-

creasing animation, putting her arms akimbo as she saw the corner of Ruth's eye open, "for keeping up the reel. I cut in and out like mad; Jim Barnstable swore I beat all; the more shame that he went and courted Sal Capers. She caper! she was just made for mincing a minuet. A mean feller he to be puttin on his ball-clothes the mornin after the frolic at Captin Wright's barn, and comin and talkin an hour to me as if his mouth was sweetened with molasses, and then to go and court Sal Capers."

Bridget had touched a very important string in Ruth's associations. She too was to receive visiters, whose discourse would, perhaps, flow with diviner nectar than Jim Barnstable's; and, raising herself on her pillow, the print of which marked her soft cheek, she asked the hour.

Ruth had once detested morning calls. It seemed hard to her to set aside her interesting occupations, and give herself up to the commonplaces of that talk which is not long enough to elicit ideas, and yet of sufficient duration to break up most valuable portions of time. But the graceful sweetness of her nature had taught her to study the happiness of others in this usually heartless ceremony. She had learned from her mother to employ herself in some light work, which, while it was a kind of rallying-point for conversation, could be thrown aside at pleasure. If she were embarrassed, her eyes found rest upon her busy fingers; and if her guests were dull, their very motion seemed a help. But Ruth gave no heed to her sewing this day; for, by the time that her truant hair was smoothed to glossiness, and her breakfast hastily despatched, she heard the gate shut to with its well-known swing, and

H

saw her two partners advancing up the foot-path to the house.

There was, indeed, no need of the needle to beguile that hour; her birds, her flowers, her books, her songs, and, most of all, her laughter over the events of the past night, inspired her guests with confidence. Frank and unselfish as Ruth was, she might have been charged with coquetry by those who did not understand her. The desire to please, springing, as it did, from the best fountains of the heart, leads to results like coquetry; while her mother feared to check her too anxiously, lest, by chilling her confidence in others, she should create an unnatural self-observation and reserve.

"Which of those two young men do *you* like best, mamma?" said Ruth, as she stood at the window, and heard the closing swing of the gate, and saw their retreating forms.

"Your emphasis implies that you have made up *your* mind about the matter," said her mother, smiling. Ruth blushed and protested. There was a pause, and Mrs. Raymond changed the conversation.

"Your enjoyment last night, and the excitement of new scenes," said she, "must not prevent your studying to be useful. I have been called upon by some ladies this morning to aid them in getting up a Sunday-school. The office assigned me is to apply to those who can afford it, to give subscriptions to purchase clothing and books for the poor scholars, and to the indigent to send their children to be instructed. My health is failing, dear, and I must make you my substitute in this benevolent project."

"Me, mamma!" exclaimed Ruth. "What *can* I

say? I shall be *so* frightened if they look cross at me."

"You must think of your duty, and that will strength-en you. You will have harder duties, Ruth, to bear when I am gone."

Ruth looked at her mother. There was a paleness on her face that made her tremble. She threw herself on a low seat beside her, and hid her face in her lap. A dread came over her that sickened her very heart, and she could not speak. Mrs. Raymond changed the current of her thoughts by entering into an explana-tion of the project, and the part Ruth was to sustain.

"Rouse yourself, my daughter," she said, affection-ately. "You must begin your expedition immediate-ly, and the pure air will do you good. Reflect on all I have taught you, and call up your own thoughts on the way."

Ruth went up stairs and mechanically tied on her bonnet. Mrs. Fry would never have claimed her as a votary of philanthrophy. Ruth thought only of her mother; but there is something in nature, in the blue heavens, and the stirring impulses of a frosty air, con-genial to the young. As her feet crushed the frozen snow, she threw care to the winds; and when she heard the gate fall to behind her, her step quickened and her eye brightened. She began to reflect on her mission, and bent her steps to farmer Morefield's, about half a mile distant. The family were just at dinner, and the farmer, wiping the cider from his mouth, asked the young lady to take a bite. Ruth declined; but having once entered on her task, her ardent character support-ed her, and she said, though with considerable tremour in her voice,

"The ladies of the village are anxious to have a Sunday-school. Should you like to subscribe and send your children?"

"I will answer about the money part," said the farmer, good-naturedly, "but my old woman will tell you about the children."

Ruth took out her subscription paper; it was modest enough; one dollar per year, and such donations as the liberal could afford. The farmer gave her a dollar.

Ruth looked at the lady, who was just pulling a huge bone from the mouth of one of the expected catechumens.

"Will it be agreeable to you to send your children to church next Sunday, at nine o'clock?" she said. "The ladies will take great pleasure in teaching them."

"I don't think, Mr. Morefield," replied the lady, without looking at Ruth, and swallowing hastily a spoonful of broth, "that we've quite come to charity yet. It's a pity if we can't keep our heads above water a *leetle* longer!"

Ruth was half tempted to get up and run; but she rallied herself, and tried to speak.

"Don't be in a passion, wife," said the farmer; "let's hear the young lady. If it's a charity business, miss, we reckon ourselves as well to live as anybody."

Ruth began with tremour, but soon went on quietly to tell the objects of the Sunday-school; the motives of teachers; the aid to parents; the pleasure to children. Warming with her subject, she related, from her past reading, one or two anecdotes of youths, whose souls, under this religious teaching, had been taught the upward way. "My own little brothers and sisters will all attend *our* school," continued Ruth, beginning to feel the spirit of prosleytism.

" Do let us go.   We want to go," said two or three of the childish group, who had been listening attentive-ly to Ruth's sweet voice, and now pressed round their mother.   "Be still, you!" said the mother.   "If it isn't charity, you may go and welcome ; and, husband, you mought as well give another dollar to help the young woman out with her business."

Ruth's eyes glistened with something like a tear as she perceived this reaction, and, taking the dollar grate-fully, she went her way with airy footsteps.   The bar-berry bushes and straggling sweet-brier seemed cloth-ed with beauty, and in the lightness of her heart she sang the song she loved.

The next building in sight was a farmhouse also, but the aspect of all things around was negligent.   The owner appeared to be trying to repair, in a rough way, an aperture in the wall, to prevent the encroachment of cattle on his premises.

Ruth went up to him timidly.   " Will you allow me, sir," she said, "to say a few words to you and your family ?"   The man looked at her hardly, and she saw the stamp of intemperance in his bloodshot eyes.

"I don't care if you do," was his gruff reply, ad-vancing, as he spoke, before her, with a tottering step, to his residence.   His wife was at the washtub, while several clamorous children were hushed at the sight of a stranger.

"Suke," said the farmer, "this young miss wants to speak to us!"   The woman wrung the water from her hands, and handed a low stool to Ruth, who sat down.

Ruth saw, by an air of patient sufferance on her face,

H 2

that she was not the person to apply to, and, turning to the farmer, said,

"Several ladies wish the children of our village to join in a Sunday class. They are to assemble at the meeting-house before the service begins, and learn the Bible and hymns. Will you allow yours to go?"

"You may put my children *in* the meetin-house or *behind* it," said the farmer, roughly. "I give 'em clothes and victuals, and that's enough."

Ruth shuddered; the *graveyard* was behind the church; but seeing the drooping, imploring-looking woman, for her sake she took courage and said,

"You cannot be serious, sir. These children want something more than food and clothing; they are God's children as well as yours."

"God may take care of them and be ——," said the farmer, fiercely.

The woman started with almost a cry, and Ruth saw, with horror, that the case was hopeless. She turned to the children, who had resumed their play, and asked a bright-looking boy if he would not like to go to meeting, and see all the little boys and girls every Sunday morning, and learn about God.

"I don't care if I do, if sister Nance goes," said the boy, scraping the wall in various fanciful patterns with a rusty nail.

"Will you go, little Nancy?" asked Ruth, following the direction of the boy's look to a pretty-eyed girl, whose matted curls fell over cheeks ruddy with health. "You shall have a nice frock and bonnet to wear on Sundays," she added, in a whisper.

"I'll go if Dick wants me to," said the girl, with an attempt at a courtesy.

The father had gone back to his work, and the mother's eye brightened.

"Dick and Nancy are willing to attend the school," said Ruth to the woman; "I am sure you will not object."

"No, God Almighty bless you, miss," said she, "but they have no clothes, and poor Hartley's earnings will not buy them any." She did not hint that poor Hartley's earnings were spent at the tavern.

"I will dress them every Sunday if you will send them to me," said Ruth. "Pray let them come. You must send them *very* early; teachers and scholars must be punctual," added she, turning with a smile to the children.

Dick, however, heard not; his rusty nail had created a ship on the wainscoat, masts, and sails, and all, and Nancy was admiring it with her eyes and mouth open. Ruth bade farewell to this little group, and was cheered on by the aid and gratitude of three thriving families whom she visited in succession.

Proceeding on her way, she saw a miserable hovel. Ruth had never entered the abodes of the really poor, and shrank dismayed. The fences were all appropriated for firewood, a ragged hat filled one of the broken panes of glass, and the accumulated dirt at the doorstep was so forbidding, that she was about turning aside from the entangled path, when the pale face of a child appeared at the door, and she remembered her mission. The child drew back as she caught the eye of a stranger, while Ruth advanced, and tapped gently and modestly on the swinging door. A noble heart feels more deep humility in approaching such a scene than at the entrance of palaces.

"Come in," said a youthful voice.

Ruth entered, and the little girl, whose face she had seen peeping from the door, stood, half screening herself amid some ragged bedding, where a man lay in the hard breathing of disease.

"Hush, father's asleep," whispered the little girl, "and mother says he mustn't be waked up till she comes back, 'cause he cries just like a baby when she ain't here."

Ruth beckoned to the little girl with a sympathizing look, and she issued shyly from her hiding-place.

"What is the matter with your father?" whispered Ruth.

"I don't know, miss; only he can't walk about, nor lift up his arms, and he don't act like a man, but takes on like a baby."

Ruth knew too little of disease to recognise one of the stages of paralysis in this description.

"I should like to help your poor father," said Ruth, in a very pitying tone, for her heart was stirred up within her. "What can I do for *you?*"

"I should like a bit of bread," said the child, "'cause mammy stays so long." The provident care of Mrs. Raymond had filled Ruth's bag with biscuits for her long ramble, and she hastily extended some to the hungry child.

"Will your father be displeased to see me here if he wakes?" said Ruth.

"No," replied the child; "he does not mind anybody but mammy and me."

"What is your name?" asked Ruth.

"Susan," was the answer.

"I will be a friend to you, Susan, if you will be a good girl. A great many little boys and girls are going to meet together, and read the Bible and learn hymns. Should you like to join them every Sunday morning ?"

" I am afraid to go anywhere without mammy," said Susan.

Ruth glanced round the miserable hut, and wondered what protection the poor little girl could feel there.

At that moment an almost inarticulate sound issued from the bed.

" Wife," at last said the sick man, with effort, his hands shaking with the disease.

Susan ran to him, and said soothingly, " Mammy's just stepped out to buy some bread ; she will be back in a minute, father."

" She's gone and left me again," mumbled the poor sufferer, in imperfect tones, and then burst into hys-terical sobs and tears.

Susan stood by helplessly, saying, " Don't cry, fa-ther, don't. Mammy will be here directly." Then, wiping the tears on his face with the tattered sheet, she said in his ear, " Don't cry, father, the pretty lady is looking at you."

Ruth could bear it no longer ; she rushed into the open air, exclaiming involuntarily, in the language of Scripture, " Merciful heaven ! *I* have bread enough and to spare, and they perish with hunger !"

CHAPTER XVII.

Ruth's Reflections at Home.—More Experiences of Human Nature.
—The Sunday-school Opens.—Ruth Compensated.

RUTH walked droopingly along the dreary outlet to the road. The landscape had lost its charm, and the sun looked dim as she glanced back on the poor dwelling, where Susan was wiping the tears from the cheeks of her imbecile parent. Collecting her thoughts, she returned through a by-path home, and poured out her full heart to her mother. There was a fitfulness of manner unusual to her as she retired that night to her tasteful and tranquil bedroom. She felt almost a jealousy of her own comforts, and sighed often, " Poor, poor Susan!" Her garments were cast aside unfolded, and no glance was thrown at the mirror to ask if her pretty nightcap sat becomingly. Before reading her Bible, she sat abstractedly on a low seat by the bedside. At length she opened its leaves. Her reading was systematic, and the appointed passages were in the Old Testament, in the abstruser parts of prophecy. Poor Ruth read on blindly, no sympathetic cord touching her heart, which was so fully strung to soft emotions. She did not throw the book aside, for it was her *Bible*, but she laid it down with another sigh. Again she took it listlessly, and her eyes fell on those touching passages in St. John's gospel, where our Saviour speaks of his own sufferings. She read on. " There must be a deep meaning in sorrow," thought she, " if *he* suffered," and she laid her head musingly on her pillow. That day had unfolded a fresh leaf in her heart's history; it was no longer an impaled butterfly that moved her sympathy; a new *love* stirred her affections, the love of her suffering fellow-creatures. Then followed hopes and resolutions for their happiness; and, falling asleep, she saw poor Susan in her dreams, no longer the pale, sad child of penury, but clothed in white robes and treading heavenly bowers.

Ruth rose in the morning refreshed in spirit, and, followed by a domestic with comforts for the sick and food for the hungry, visited again Susan's abode. The child, won over by her kindness, promised to attend the Sabbath-school; and Ruth appointed the old school-house as a place of rendezvous for those who were to accompany her home, to be measured for their new dresses that day. Her success in the more populous parts of the village was fluctuating; but jealousy and coldness were the predominant feelings, until the warmth of her own manner conquered them, and brought out the latent tenderness which lies in every heart where the right depth is sounded. Almost invariably the women referred her to their husbands for the *dollar*. The disciples of the Female Liberty-school may sneer at this very marked feature in our domestic manners, well-known by those who have solicited subscriptions, but to me there is nothing ridiculous about it; it implies sympathy in conjugal life; it checks the too great tendency to overflow in female benevolence, and aids economy; for if a woman discusses one dollar with her husband, she will have some insight into his hundreds.

Entering one house, Ruth saw a woman of plain, quiet manners, with two children, and unfolded her ob-

ject in visiting her. She was answered by warm and
pious sympathy, and not only sympathy in words, but
the woman, with a tear in her eye, handed her a ten-
dollar note, wishing blessings on the cause. Ruth was
fairly startled; scarcely able to utter her thanks in her
delighted surprise, she wrapped the treasure up with
care, and went to the old schoolhouse where the children were to assemble to accompany her home. A
goodly number were there, but such a looking crew!
Poor Ruth, in ordering the line of march, could only
distinguish them as the little girl with the ragged apron,
or the boy without the hat, or her with the toes out at
her shoes, or him without any shoes. Little Susan
she took by the hand. Utterly forgetful of the appearance she must make with this " ragged regiment," she
proceeded homeward, talking with Susan as freely as
if it had been Isabel by her side, until she was recalled
to the circumstance by the appearance of two gentlemen on the road. Ruth looked back with some dis-
may; two of her protégés were snowballing each other,
and the blood, streaming from the nose of one of these
knights-errant, testified to the prowess of his opponent.
Two others, very little girls, had rambled off to gather
some lingering apples in an open orchard; and Susan,
beginning to be home-sick and frightened, put her
apron to her eyes to wipe away the tears. Ruth, at
her wits' end, scarcely knew whether to divide the com-
batants, or reclaim the wanderers, or sooth Susan. In
the midst of her embarrassments, Clarendon and William drew near. Ruth wavered a moment, and would
willingly have screened herself by a neighbouring tree,
and allowed them to pass; but her frank good-humour
conquered. Greeting them modestly, she told her sim-

ple perplexities and asked their aid.   This was, in reality, but a picturesque spectacle, contrasted as the beautiful and graceful Ruth was with these children of poverty.   But Ruth and the young men had human weaknesses; and, when one or two carriages rolled by, they shrunk back, or raised a compliment of forced laughter, or waved off the little group to a wider distance; still, in spite of its singularity, the scene had its charms for the new actors.   The embarrassment of Ruth was not awkward; her sunny temper broke out even more gayly amid the strong contrasts about her; and the aspect of one so young and fair, employed in a work of *love* for poor humanity, told a tale that went down deep into the hearts of the two warm-souled youths, who aided her in marshalling her restless retinue, and, by promises of cake and sugar-plums, stimulated their erratic movements.

"Mamma," said Ruth, with a rather consequential air, before a committee which met for the purpose of arranging the school on the following morning, "do you not think the ladies should return a vote of thanks to Mrs. Bedloe for the ten dollars she gave me?"

"Certainly, Ruth," said her mother; and Ruth was requested by the committee to write and send it.

She sat down and bit the end of her pen.   "What a miserable cold thing a letter of thanks is," she thought, "when one's heart is full!   I wish they would let me run down the lane and thank her."

The note at length was written, and submitted in form; its ardency suppressed, moulded to a committee dignity, and sent.   The messenger soon returned with the reply that the house was unoccupied, and Mrs. Bedloe had left town.

I

Ruth burst into raptures. "How disinterested! No common mind," she said, "would have given thus without any prospect of a return. Mamma," she said, growing sentimental, "such charity is like the sun, which throws his careless beams on every little flower; and to think that I was the medium of this benevolence!"

As Ruth thus vented her feelings, Mr. Raymond, who had been absent, entered. Springing towards him, she narrated the circumstance, and showed him the ten-dollar note.

"The rascals!" exclaimed her father, "Bedloe is a forger, and absconded last night. Tear up the bill, child, it is good for nothing!"

Ruth sank into a chair speechless as that first lesson of depravity was discovered, then she wept, then grew indignant.

"I will not subject myself to such impositions again," she said, angrily. "I shall never think well of human nature after this. That cold, heartless, smiling, sycophantic wretch of a woman, I wish she was obliged to eat the bill," she continued, as she tore it in pieces.

Fortunately for Ruth, her time was busily occupied in making the Sunday garments for the children; and, before the week was closed, she observed so much quiet good feeling and Christian kindness among the ladies with whom she was associated as to reconcile her to human nature again.

Sunday was a proud day for Ruth. The "ragged regiment" was converted into a respectable procession. It is true she laboured more over the physical than moral purity of her protégés; but perhaps she was jus-

tified by scripture, which recommends " clean hands"
before a " pure heart."

The old pastor delivered a touching discourse on the
opening of the Sabbath-school. He praised and blessed the zeal of modern Christians, who identify the religious interests of youth with their own, and he called
upon the little children to be ready to join him in the
great school of Heaven, where, if they were all good,
they would be pupils in God's everlasting lessons of
love with him.

A hymn was then sung, and the children who could
be taught in so short a space joined their " small
voice ;" then a contribution was announced to be received, and four teachers took each by the hand a little scholar, who, with a small basket, advanced to the
several pews. Ruth led Susan, and earnestly pushed
forward her little hand, forgetting the publicity of the
scene in her sympathy with the child. It was difficult
not to give those two more than one meant to. Ruth,
trembling, sparkling, glowing, pleaded with her lustrous innocent eyes, while the blue orbs of the pale-
faced girl were upturned only to her.

As Ruth was counting her treasure as soon after the
benediction as decency allowed, her eyes fell on a bright
gold piece ; it was ten dollars, and no forgery ! Ruth's
memory told her when a metallic sound unlike the rest
was heard over the little basket.

CHAPTER XVIII.

The Sleigh-ride.—An Overturn.—Excitement.—William a Rich Man.—An Offer of Marriage.

MANY a cheek glowed and many an eye glistened as sleigh after sleigh stopped with jingling bells one fine evening at Mr. Raymond's gate for a moonlight ride. Ruth, wrapped in her furs, stood ready, and sprang into that which was occupied by Doctor Gesner and Isabel. William, who held the reins, extended his hand, and gently but forcibly drew her to the seat beside him, while Clarendon wrapped her in the buffalo skin, placed the heated bricks at her feet, and took his seat with Isabel and the doctor behind them.

The order was given, and the jocund train passed on, skimming the sheeted road like birds.

There was not a cloud in the sky; the magnificent moon trod her unimpeded way, a very queen, showering down a flood of radiance, kindling up the meanest things with order and loveliness, and harmonizing every snow-clad bough and blade as they quivered diamond-like in the sea of light. The river, bound in frost, lay still; the rustle of the trees was still; man and beast were still; all was silence save the song and laugh that went up from that glancing group. Silvery and sweet it rose on the quiet air, and the moon, as she listened in her complacent love, looked down on the light-hearted ones with such a ray as bewitched Endymion.

A sleigh-ride offers many opportunities for gentle courtesies. William, who was oceans deep in love,

felt his naturally gay humour soften down to a worship-
ping tenderness. The moonlight was doubly fair to
him, because it dwelt on Ruth, and gave a halo-bright-
ness to her beaming face as she sat beside him.

" Do you remember, Miss Raymond," he whispered, " our first interviews ?"

" Yes," answered Ruth, laughing, " we were at opposite sides of the street ; a very pleasant kind of intercourse with some people."

" Oh, Miss Raymond," said the youth, falteringly,
" trifle not when all around is so earnest and real.
Flatter me with *seriousness,* and leave jest for daylight
and the world."

Ruth was confused by his earnestness ; and, as he
leaned towards her to catch her reply, it was not surprising that he should guide his horses on a tremeu-
dous snowdrift, and upset his precious cargo, while the
steeds passed on at an easy gallop. Dr. Gesner was
the first to roll out, and incontinently descend to the
foot of the hill, where he slowly rose with unintelligible
gutturals, and stood square and stiff like a snowman
made by schoolboys. Isabel had been aided by a gentleman who sprang from the sleigh behind. Clarendon offered no assistance to Ruth ; he stood at a little
distance, with folded arms, in silence ; a change had
passed over his spirit. William was near her. His
heart throbbed as he drew her hand within his arm ;
and as he poured out his wild poetic rhapsodies, Ruth
forgot that good Doctor Gesner was hobbling towards
them, and that Clarendon was walking musingly alone.
She was agitated and almost alarmed. Was it *love*
that made her tremble and be silent, or the novelty of
inspiring love ?

When Ruth reached home, she retreated to her own apartment, and trod the floor again and again in revery.

"He said he was poor," she murmured. "Can there be poverty where there is such wealth of mind and heart?   And is it possible that *I*, with a word, a look, can make him happy?   Poor William! I hope he *will* be happy."

The next morning, as she sat at work with her mother, a letter was brought her, which she hastily unfolded.   Mrs. Raymond looked up from her sewing ; tears were rolling down Ruth's cheeks ; but scarcely had they fallen before a shout of laughter followed, and Ruth absolutely hid her face on the table to hide her hysterical convulsions, as she handed her the following lines.

 " Miss Raymond,

"Was I right in the indications of last evening ? Am I beloved?   Then I had no authority to ask the question.   I was a poor man struggling for an honourable livelihood.   Now I have wealth, but what is wealth if the affections are poor ?   Even at this moment, when a sudden reverse of fortune has made me affluent, I feel that one answered pulsation from your heart would be worth a thousand worlds.   You will think me dreaming.   It seems to me almost that I am.   Heaven knows that I shall wish I were without your smiles.   Listen to me, and answer ; yet oh delay, if the answer be not what my soul alone sighs for.   On returning from our excursion last evening, I found a letter from the exec utor of my maternal uncle, who has died, leaving me an immense fortune on the easy condition that I take his name. How can I show my devotion better than by laying this wealth at your feet? Take it, dearest Miss Raymond, with a heart that beats only to serve you, a hand whose only pride will be to protect you; and which, though no longer using the signature of William White, is equally yours as

" WILLIAM PIPE."

Ruth peeped through her fingers at her mother, who vainly attempted to preserve her gravity.

" I am a fool, mamma, I know I am," said Ruth, struggling with her risible tendencies, and wiping her tears at the same time, " to be such a victim of the ludicrous. I had no sooner read that name, than the idea of Mrs. Ruth Pipe came into my head and choked me with laughter. I am afraid I was a little in love with William last night, he was so eloquent and yet so delicate; but I am cured. It could not have been love either, because," and here she burst into renewed laughter, " because, if I really had loved—'a rose by any other name,' &c.—you know, mamma."

The hardest task Ruth ever performed was to write a serious answer to that letter; and, when it was finished, Mrs. Raymond perceived that she had listlessly scribbled on a blank sheet of paper, in the interim of writing each sentence, " Ruth Pipe!" " Mrs. Ruth Pipe!"

Ruth was not in *love*.

CHAPTER XIX.

Ruth's Grotto.—A Sister's Love.—New Sensations.

WINTER has passed away. The last mimic ava-
lanche has glided down the mountains, and the little
rills fall at their feet, whose exhalations, tinged with
countless hues of beauty, rise up and roll off amid cc-
rulean depths. A bird, Ruth thinks it is the same
that has greeted her for three years, sings on her apple-tree bough near the wall. Ruth is thoughtful with
joy, to see the snowdrop that peers up in smiles amid
the waste of her garden. You remember the rustic
bridge leading to the mill, where she chased the butterfly. Ruth hastened thither with her youngest sister, to see what nature had done there. The stream
was flowing merrily, blades of grass were springing,
and the rush of waters on the mill-wheel brought
back, as sounds so often do, sweet memories. Near
the bridge, a semicircular rock made, and concealed
too, what Ruth called her grotto. A maple-tree slant-
ed from the river bank above it, and shrubbery, rising
below and around, shut out its interior from the very
few wanderers who chanced to visit her father's
grounds. Here she had floated her mimic boats—
poor, girlish efforts—chips with riband sails ; here she
had brought her dolls, placing Miss Beauty on the softest moss, and made for the inanimate group an entertainment of mud puddings. As time advanced, she
found this spot still more favourable than her apple-
tree-seat to study and to music ; now she sought it for

reflection. The dry leaves, whirled to the enclosure by autumnal winds, were piled up within; and, placing her little sister on a stone at the entrance, too high for her to reach herself, she began gathering them up in her hands, and throwing them into the river. Little Rosalie quietly watched her sister's busy motions, and murmuring something like a tune, kept time by knocking her suspended feet against the stone, while Ruth, as she passed from distributing her gathered leaves, stole a kiss from the child's white forehead.

Her labour was nearly completed, when, as she stooped to gather up the leaves in the farthest recess, her hand touched something cold, and a large black-snake reared itself almost to her very face; then rapidly sinking and retreating, coiled itself near a shrub, where a bed of withered leaves yet remained between herself and Rosalie. Unconscious of the vicinity of the reptile, the child kept on singing her broken snatches of infantile tunes until startled by Ruth's sudden cry of alarm.

"Run, Rosalie, run away!" she exclaimed, fearing to move, lest the reptile should glide towards the child.

Rosalie looked wonderingly at her sister, but moved not.

"Go, dear little sister! go away, go away, Rosalie, for God's sake!" and Ruth's voice rose to a shriek of terror, for she dreaded that the snake, though fearful of man, might attack the child. Rosalie extended her arms to her sister and ceased her song. Ruth looked round for some offensive weapon; none presented itself; the slight shrubbery that sprang about the fissures of the rock was all that met her eye; at length one object arrested her attention. At a jutting point of the rock above the serpent, she saw a loose fragment of stone; and, deliberately calculating its distance from Rosalie, without thinking of her own risk, she decided to attempt the ascent and throw it down. *Love* led her on. With a motion as soft as that around the bed of a dear slumberer, she unfastened her slippers from her feet, and clinging, with an almost convulsive grasp, to the first slight projection, sprang to a broader ledge. Rosalie resumed her song. Ruth looked up in doubt; the maple leaned just above her; one single step more, and she could reach it with her hand; but there was no step; she must spring up towards it, or lose her only hope. Rosalie still sang, and her sweet, happy notes nerved a sister's *love*. Planting her foot firmly on the ledge, she leaped upward; the maple branch was attained with one hand; a vibratory swing brought her body against the top of the rock; she bent one instant upon it, then, with a spasmodic effort, threw herself above. Panting, she looked below. The snake, disturbed by the rustling, began to uncoil. Rosalie sang on. Ruth hastened to the rocky fragment, looked once more cautiously below, then thrust both hands against it. It fell. Ruth closed her eyes dizzily. She had never harmed a fly before, life was so dear to her. She did not look again, but hastened down the river bank to the entrance of her grotto. The stone had fallen surely. A part of the mangled reptile quivered in sight. Rosalie, frightened and wondering, held out her arms to Ruth, who took the child in her own, nor spake a word, nor gave her one caress, until she had passed out of sight of the rock; then kissing her with tumultuous joy, she threw herself on the ground as weak as infancy.

That spot, sacred before to Ruth, became doubly so

now; but it was several days before she had courage
to visit it, and then with a thoughtful, grateful heart, she
went and paused at the entrance.   But what a change!
the withered leaves of autumn were all carefully removed; beautiful mosses decorated the rough interior;
and a bouquet of greenhouse flowers was thrown on
her favourite seat.   She searched busily around; to
common eyes, no sign appeared to tell the author of
this delicate and graceful tribute to her feelings; but
as she gazed in silence, a rich blush rose mantling on
her cheek; on and on it went, over forehead, and neck,
and arms; a smile dimpled round her mouth; a sigh,
full, soft, and blissful, rushed up from her heart's depths;
a dewy brightness glittered on her eyes.   She took the
flowers in her hand, and a thrill from their odorous
beauty stole through her frame.   She pressed them to
her lips, she murmured a name amid their leaves.
There was no witness, no listener; the secret of that
throbbing heart was all its own.

CHAPTER XX.

Delicate Positions.—Ruth's Character unfolds.—Glimpses into Hearts.

"You have been so eloquent about this law-case of your father's, that I almost wish it was yours, and, more than that, I wish I were a man to hear it," said Ruth Raymond, as Clarendon and herself leaned on the low railing of the foot-bridge, alternately looking up, as the sun, wrapped in gorgeous drapery, rolled to the west, and downward on the reflected image of the heavens in the stream.   Every object was as clearly defined below as above; the shading of every leaf on the bending trees, the moss on the rocks, the slightest cloud, were all brought to the lower picture with an almost startling distinctness.

"If I *am* called upon, I shall pray as to a patron saint," said Clarendon, "for such inspiration as *you* could give."

Two thirds of the power of this remark lay in its emphasis; and Ruth, who usually looked full in the face of those who addressed her, found occasion to watch intently some rose-leaves which she had torn to pieces and thrown into the stream.

"Poor rose-leaves!" murmured Clarendon, in a tone that, in the stillness, just reached her ear as she bowed over the railing; "Ruth Raymond throws you away!'

Clarendon could not see her face, for her hair fell about her cheek and shaded it; so he bent over the railing, and Ruth became conscious that he was gazing in the glassy surface below, to see her image reflected there.

" You need not pity the rose-leaves," she said, care-lessly, " for they have found a nice Ruth Raymond in the water; and look, Mr. Clarendon! the reflection of that dark purple cloud is an exact likeness of old Dr. Gesner too; his capacious mouth, his huge shoul-ders, with a supplementary ornament of farmer Mans-field's queue by way of finish!"

The words that had been welling up from Clarendon's heart of hearts were thrust back; he surrendered his earnest, truthful mood with a sigh, and the hope of re-newing a subject to which Ruth's ardent expression of interest in his success had given rise, was crushed by the appearance of Dr. Gesner, no shadow.

" Why is that young man idling here?" said Mr. Raymond, who approached as Clarendon departed.

" You do him great injustice, papa," said Ruth, indig-nantly. " He has been preparing himself for several weeks to assist his infirm father as junior counsel in the case of Leeds and Whittesby."

" And he comes to read law in your eyes, Ruth, eh?"

" No, sir," said Ruth, very gravely; " Mr. Clarendon has not been to the village for two weeks; and he came to-day, after a bewildering examination into legal ref-crences, exhausted by midnight study, with the hope that the sight of calm and beautiful nature might re-fresh him. He trembles for his father's reputation, since the old gentleman persists in conducting the case himself, and, besides, is agitated at the prospect of his first effort. He could not have had a more inspiring evening than this," continued Ruth, glad to escape to the portico, where the long twilight glimmered through the tree-tops, while fantastic shapes were revealed in the shrubbery below. Tempted by the scene, she strayed down the gravel-walk, and gave herself up to a rapturous adoration of nature.

Keeping the parlour lights in view, she went no farther than her apple-tree bough. Singing to herself, and looking upward, to see star after star marshalled above, she was disturbed by hearing some one leap the wall. She started, but without alarm. It might be the gardener, and she simply asked who was there.

"It is I," said Clarendon, with some embarrassment. "As I was about to enter the boat, the young moon stood so serene and quiet among the hill-tops, that I could not resist asking you to see it *with me ;* so I took the shortest path back, and, hearing your voice, sprang over the wall."

Ruth's heart fluttered like a frightened bird; but she rallied herself, and said quietly,

"The moon has behaved as all discreet ladies ought, and gone to rest; and let me tell you a secret, Mr. Clarendon. I have been obliged to defend you against a charge of idleness with all my dignity since your departure, and used up a part of the eloquent speech you made me about recreating your overtasked mind among the works of nature. What excuse shall I give for *this* romantic movement ?" and, as she spoke, she turned towards the house.

"I scarcely know or care," said Clarendon, throwing himself on the mound by her side, and gently detaining her scarf. "Believe me, that, for the last fortnight, my imagination amid the drudgery of the office has revelled only in halls of legislation. I have been grappling with gigantic shadows, while the wish for

usefulness and fame was paramount to every other desire. I did come here, in truth, to be soothed and refreshed by nature, after undue excitement; but one look
of yours, an unconscious look too, changed my whole
being. Ruth, Miss Raymond, if I could see *once* more
the expression that was reflected in the stream this
evening! Oh for one ray of light to tell me if it is
now the same."

There *was* no light to tell whether those intellectual
eyes were softened to tenderness, whether even tears
did not stand on their fringed lids ; no light to tell if a
dimpling smile of conscious triumph mocked the tears ;
and what if the silken scarf which Clarendon held fluttered more than it was wont over that young bosom ?
Was not the western wind at work amid its folds ?

Ruth had an innate sense of propriety, that invariably pointed the right way in action, though her words
might sometimes too much overflow. Gentle but firm
was her voice as she answered,

" This is not the hour or place, Mr. Clarendon, for
expressions like yours. The appearance of a clandes-
tine meeting is revolting to me. Besides, you are ca-
pricious to-night. At sunset the law was your lady-
love, next the new moon crazed you, and now you are
looking in the dark for an expression that went under
the mill with the tide an hour ago. Good-night; a
sunshiny day and a righteous judge for your cause."

Clarendon's was that first, timid, doubting love which
a word can repulse. He retreated in silence, but Ruth
knew that he pressed the fringe of her scarf to his lips
as she drew it from him. She heard him leap the wall,
and felt dizzy and faint as she retraced her steps on
the gravelled walk. Seated in the parlour, sights and

sounds seemed floating about her like visions. Once or twice it appeared to her that soft music was near. her; the other members of the circle, however, only heard Dr. Gesner, who was overcome by a long chase after a dragon-fly, snore.

Clarendon drew a long breath, stood erect, looked up to the stars, and, like a good ship after a lee-lurch, righted himself and darted on his way. It was rare that he gave himself up to impulse ; and, after a rapid walk, he began to fear that he had been extra-sentiment- al, to go two miles to ask a young lady to see a moon which was setting among the hilltops, to say nothing of looking in her eyes in the dark for an expression he had seen in the water, the most distorting and ex- aggerating of elements. He diligently renèwed his studies on the morrow ; and, if he sometimes looked up from a brief, as a haunting smile, a floating curl, a happy footstep, or a thrilling tone came on his memo- ry, who shall blame him, since he often said to himself, "She is guileless ; she is a respectful, tender child; a considerate sister, a bright, warm-hearted companion ; her hopes are heavenward, she is the sunshine of her home! I will do something worthy of Ruth Raymond!"

CHAPTER XXI.

Ruth's Singing.—A Letter.—The case of Leeds and Whittesby.—
Ruth Weeps.—A Denouément expected.

"It was fresh and laughing June," as Mrs. Raymond, her pale hand guiding her needle, sat in the same shaded parlour where Ruth whispered her first juvenile secrets; and though the bloom and elasticity of her youth were gone, the grace of matronly dignity, a tenderness that looked with love on a fading world, was thrown around her. No harsh repining or doubt impressed its tone on her features. It seemed that as the landscape of life grew dim, the colours were softened; as the waters reached the precipice, they became more smooth.

Ruth entered with a sheet of music paper, and stumbling over Perdita, now a patriarch among the cats, sat down to the piano, laughing at her own awkwardness. A very trifle often brings up a long train of associations, and this laugh carried Mrs. Raymond far back; it was so fresh, and young, and childlike, that she looked up at Ruth almost expecting to see the little form and tossing hair of the rope-skipper of seven; but the laugh had ceased, and the mother recognised in the modelled form, and the chaste and elevated expression, her more matured child. Ruth was singing "Here awa' there awa' wandering Willie," the exquisite tenderness of which was suited perfectly to the character of her voice. Mrs. Raymond's heart thrilled,

K 2

and her eyes were moistened, as, with a distinct, impassioned utterance, almost like recitative, she sang,

"Winter winds blew cauld and loud at our parting,
  Fears for my Willie brought tears to my e'e ;
Welcome now simmer, and welcome my Willie,
  The simmer to nature, my Willie to me."

Mrs. Raymond had a faith that voices would not be
lost.   I shall hear those tones again, she whispered to
herself, sublimated, refined, among angel choirs.

Ruth was interrupted by a servant with a large
packet.

"It is from Isabel at New-York, mamma," she
said, starting up, breaking the seal.   As she glanced
at the first page, a deep blush suffused her face, and she
stood embarrassed.

"·I should like to read this letter alone," she then
said, hurriedly ; and giving her mother a kind of apol-
ogetic kiss, ran quickly down the garden path to her
grotto.

The reader and I can peep over her shoulder.

"In a quiet corner at the end of your double letter,
dearest Ruth, which is filled with such a glorious description of your sunsets, such excellent criticisms on
Gibbon, and such valid arguments on the propriety of
young ladies studying logic, I find this question : 'Do
you think Mr. Clarendon will be called upon to speak
in the Leeds and Whittesby case ?'

"As this is the *only* question in your three pages,
I feel bound to answer it at large.

"Clarendon has spoken, and is the lion of the day.
To say the truth, I did not expect he would be a good
orator on the nonce, he is so singularly quiet, advances
his opinions with such modesty, and has so little en-

thusiasm of character." (Here Ruth smiled somewhat roguishly.) " But father, who is not easily moved, came home last night in raptures with him. The circumstances were these : Old Mr. Clarendon, who is almost superannuated, is very tenacious of his legal reputation, and cannot bear an insinuation of decay, undertook the case. His son accompanied him to the courthouse, and sustained him by quiet but adroit at-tentions. As he watched every look and motion of his father, who is somewhat deaf, no one suspected that his mental eye was fixed steadfast and keen on the oppo-site counsel, who, having opened the process with spirit, clearness, and grace, propitiated the favour of the judge, secured the attention of the audience, and made his client half a head taller with sudden hope.

" As old Mr. Clarendon arose to reply, that change was perceptible which follows when an animated and forcible speaker gives place to a prosing one. Re-spect for his character and past services at the bar preserved the court from any open manifestations ; but the uneasy motion, the half encouraged cough, the crumpled papers, the outstretched foot scraping on the sandy floor, gave ample testimony to the presence of a tolerated bore. Matters stood thus for about a quarter of an hour, when suddenly the old man's strength failed, and he sank into a seat panting and exhausted. Clarendon gave him one keen glance of inquiry, and then rose gracefully and unhesitatingly in his place. He dwelt for a few moments respectfully and tenderly on his father's position and his own, then entered at once the mazes of litigation. His voice, you know, Ruth, is almost feminine ; but father says it swelled to such a noble distinctness that no word was lost ; a bright clear spot flushed his usually pale cheeks, and his dark eyes (so soft with us, Ruth) flashed with earnestness and intellectual power. Father says he could think of nothing so much like him as the sun rising amid clouds. Mist after mist rolled off, and left his argument and his case clear as a summer noon. And then it was so affecting to see the old man. Recovering gradually, his feeble form sat erect, but a kind of surprise, as if awakening from a dream, came over him; then placing his hand behind his ear, and leaning forward, he listened intently as a Delphian priest to the ancient oracles; then gaining strength, stood up, his white hair falling forward; he then clinched the side of his coat next his heart, as if to keep it still; twice he almost gasped for breath, still oftener passed his handkerchief over his eyes, and then, growing careless of observation, he let the large tears roll unheeded down his cheek. The plea was closed, and as a congratulating murmur arose, Clarendon turned round to the old man, who still stood as if listening, and whispered,

" ' Shall I accompany you home ?'

" ' God be thanked !' was the only reply ; and as the father and son went out, a new murmur of approbation passed round.

"I cannot tell you, my dear Ruth, any of the technicalities of the case, but I know that it is gained outright, and that Clarendon's first fee will enable him to carry a fine stock of sugarplums to little Rosalie."

After reading this letter Ruth threw her handkerchief over her face, and leaned her head against the rock.   A sweet but mighty stream was rushing over her whole soul.

" It is of no use to struggle," she said, starting up ; " I must have my cry out !" and weep she did, with the sobbing thoroughness of a spoiled child.

Relieved by this indulgence, she bathed her eyes at the river bank, and returning to her mother, gave her the letter.   That evening Mr. Raymond read aloud at the teatable the report of the case of Leeds and Whittesby, and Ruth had the rich joy of hearing Clarendon's praises from her father's lips.   A letter of the softest embossed paper accompanied the newspaper from the office, which Mr. Raymond handed to Ruth. It contained only a few words.

" Will you be in your grotto to-morrow afternoon at five o'clock ?   Tell your parents that I ask this favour.   ALFRED CLARENDON."

Ruth passed the letter to her father, who read and handed it to her mother.   There was a smile from one and a nod from the other, and no one spoke ; but Ruth knew that she *might* go to the grotto ; and so, laying the letter next her heart, she fell into divers reveries.

CHAPTER XXII.

The Interview.—A Thunder-storm.—Ruth a Creature to be Loved.

RUTH came from the toilet for the challenged interview simple and pure as the blossom that waits the
morning sun.   The slight vanity that might have en-
ticed her to linger at her mirror gave place to a more
absorbing sentiment.   She heeded not the glow that
gathered on her cheek, nor felt the airy motion with
which she trod, nor marked the tremulous lustre of the
eyes that turned mechanically to smooth the wave of
her glossy hair.   She longed for solitude ; and hastening, with unaffected directness, to the grotto before the
appointed hour, seated herself with her fingers between
the leaves of a book.   But her mind was not there ;
the rustle of the trees, the rush of the mill-wheel startled her ; now she paced the limited area of her rocky
enclosure, now impatiently looked abroad, where the
waters glittered through the hanging branches ; but,
when a real footstep approached, gathered up her maid-
en dignity, and sat collected and demure.

Clarendon came, and in a moment was seated on the
low stone at her feet.   Glad was he to see the changing colour flit over her expressive face, glad at the
tremour that parted her vainly-compressed lips.

" May I call you Ruth while I tell you the story of
my heart ?" he whispered.

" You *may* call me Ruth," was the reply.

" May I hold this hand as a pledge that you will
hear me patiently ?" he added.

The hand was not withdrawn, and for a while Clarendon could *not* speak. It seemed enough to him to
feel that treasure within his grasp. He gazed upon
it, smoothed its soft surface, and then laid his forehead against it, that its throbbings might be calmed.

" You had a story of your heart to tell me," said
Ruth, falteringly.

Clarendon raised his eyes to hers. There must have
been inspiration in those full-fringed orbs, for his words
burst forth with an energy that called up Ruth's blushes and tears in struggling mastery—such tears as can
only *once* be shed—the rainbow tears of a young heart
whose new happiness is too intense for smiles.

. And there, in the simplicity of nature, with earth for
their altar and heaven for their witness, were they
pledged together for weal or wo. May I look longer
on that scene ? The robin that whistled on the peach-
tree bough above them told not the tale in song ; the
grasshopper, vibrating on the emerald shaft at their
feet, hummed not the story to his mate ; the fish that
sprang upward in the transparent stream, went down
again in considerate silence to the pebbly bottom ;
and even a twinkling-eyed toad, whose home was in a
corner of the grotto, raised his jewelled head, and then
leaped reverently away.

An hour passed by, and the lovers saw not the cloud
that was rolling above the hills, nor heard the rever-
berating harbinger of a summer shower. The little
spot that enclosed them was the world, lit by the sunshine of their loving eyes ; and, before they suspected
the coming evil, a gleam of vivid lightning filled the
grotto, a burst of thunder shook the rock, and a gush
of winds rent the beech-tree above them. A messen-

ger came rapidly from the house to aid their return;
but Clarendon deemed it most safe to remain under the
protection of the rock until the brunt of the storm sub-
sided.   Wrapping Ruth tenderly in a cloak, and bracing an umbrella strongly over her, he perhaps felt
glad that the elementary war without thus threw her
under his protection.

"*Life* will have its storms, my own Ruth," he said,
" and thus shall I protect you, and thus will you glad-
den me."

And Ruth became assured amid the tempest.   The
almost troubled joy of her heart was hushed ; the re-
lation in which she stood to Clarendon assumed a
quiet confidence, and she turned to him as her guar-
dian.   The lightning played round her, and she stood
bright and calm as a chiselled column ; the thunder
groaned and echoed from summit to summit, but her
voice sounded silvery clear in the tumult of the elements.

A few large drops fell from the clouds, then the va-
pours rapidly parted, and the cerulean sky looked gloriously through ; gradually the winds sank to rest, the
thunder told a muttering story among the distant valleys, a rainbow arched the hills, and the western sun,
robed like a conqueror, stood a moment seemingly still,
then sank in flashing honours to repose.

As Clarendon and Ruth passed from the grotto, he
drew her gently to the bridge.   They bent a moment
over the railing together, but the agitated waters gave
back no look of love.   Did no sad presentiment tell
them that thus the stream of their affections might be
darkened and ruffled by an overruling destiny ? that
a more fearful storm might rend those hearts on which

life's sunshine seemed to rest so proudly? No such doubt was with them. There needed no mirror now to give Ruth's expression to her lover's eye. Her confiding smile made its free, untrammelled confession.

And who might stand more erect than they amid life's sunshine? A pure and righteous love united them, wealth and the world's regard were before them, beauty and manliness their dower. They hastened homeward for their crowning joy, the parental blessing, and Ruth, as she was pressed in her parents' arms, and saw her lover welcomed like a son to their affections, thought that earth could give nothing more of bliss.

"Mr. Clarendon," said Mrs. Raymond, in a softened tone, as he bade her good-night, and stood lingering beside Ruth, "I know that you feel the value of such a treasure as my child has given you in herself. I know you will love and cherish her; but forgive the thought that grows spiritual as earth fades away. Remember that, in the better world to which I am hastcuing, I shall ask for my child." And as she said this, her eye glanced upward from Ruth's bending form to heaven.

Touched and subdued by her gentle solemnity, Clarendon took the hand of his betrothed, and vowed, as he valued his own soul, to guide hers to her spiritual home.

It was a perpetual surprise to Clarendon to study, as time flew by, the development of Ruth's character and charms; the heart-gayety that sent its happy flashes into the family circle; the soberer thought that could appreciate his graver tone; the refined taste that seemed instinctively to choose whatever was of the purest texture in books, in society, in nature; the

L

beauty that now sparkled and glowed in her brilliant
cheeks and eyes, now softened to pensiveness on her
shading lids ; the songs, once for the many, now for
him, which came forth from her lips, not like a written
melody, but as a bird would sing, soul-taught ; those
motions, graceful, pliant, home-like, that accompanied
the presented flower, the dancing-step, the broken song,
the unstudied recitation of a poet's lay ; and lovelier
still, the moral growth, the indignant burst against all
that was base ; the lofty, enthusiastic love of goodness ;
the very faults of precipitation, that called up blushes
and tears in atonement ; all these Clarendon was allowed to trace from day to day in a few stolen hours
of love, and who shall say how much their memory illuminated the dry pages of legal lore, or softened the
dusty details of the courtroom ?

CHAPTER XXIII.

A Cloud on Ruth's Happiness.—A Promise.—Death.

RUTH was aroused from this spell of happiness by a mysterious depression in her mother. She had been accustomed to see in her an appearance of delicacy and debility, and had watched her for the last year with peculiar care, placing her chair in the warmest or coolest spot, supporting her arm through the garden-walks, and studying all those tender arts that a kind sensibility engenders. But this debility was accompanied by a cheerfulness that seemed the spontaneous growth of a happy heart, as well as the offspring of a religious trust. She was the playmate of her children, a companion for all. Now a change had certainly, sadly come ; and one day, when Ruth perceived that she had been weeping, she resolved delicately, but carefully, to study the change in this precious being.

"You are not anxious about papa's cough now," said Ruth.' "I never knew him so gay. He seems growing young again."

"Yes," said Mrs. Raymond, bending over her work, "he is in unusual spirits. I hope he will travel in the spring."

"With you, mamma ?" said Ruth, anxiously ; "you seem very feeble."

Mrs. Raymond looked up with a serious but serene expression, which seemed to say, "There will be no spring for me in this world."

"I wish I could feel *sure* that you are happy," said Ruth, tenderly; "I have feared lately that you were not. If *I* had a sorrow, I would tell it *all* to you. And why should you not be happy? We are all in health; papa is as gay as a boy" (Ruth did not perceive a slight shudder pass over her mother's delicate frame), "and I—you must sympathize in *my* hopes."

"God knows, my child," said Mrs. Raymond, "my gratitude for his mercies, and chiefly that he has blessed you with Clarendon's love. I look forward to your connexion with him with perpetual hope, and consign you to him as to an angel-messenger to lead you to heaven."

This sweet and tender sentiment led Ruth off from her mother's feelings to her own, and the cloud seemed to fade away from both. A few weeks passed away happily to Ruth. Her father had thrown off a natural reserve of manner, and was singularly communicative and facetious. One day, however, at dinner, in a pause of conversation, Ruth looked up at him, and saw his eyes fixed on her mother with an intensity amounting to ferocity. As Ruth looked, the expression changed, and he laughed out abruptly and painfully, while her mother turned very pale. It was strange. Ruth felt her blood curdle, but her mother smiled her gentle, tranquil smile, and all seemed as before. But that look haunted Ruth for days, and once she dreamed that her father fixed it on her until she became rigid and was turned to stone. At length that too passed away, and love and hope outgrew the stranger-plant of fear. If Mrs. Raymond had a sorrow peculiarly her own, she bore her cross in secret, in secret wore her crown of thorns, while Ruth was ignorant and happy.

But the springtime of earth was not to blossom for Mrs. Raymond. First the sunshiny walk was given up, then her chair by the parlour fire was vacated, then she could no longer lean on Ruth's arm to see the sunset from her window, nor tend the geraniums that stood with quiet leaves as if they knew her hand. The children trod round her bedside on tiptoe; but Mr. Raymond's step was hurried and bustling, unlike the leisurely step of former years. At length a chill east wind brought on a fever, and she knew that she must die.

Ruth was by her bedside at twilight, a solemn hour at any time, but chiefly so when death's shadows are gathering over one we love. There was no sound but the wind moaning without, the irregular crackling of the fire, the monotonous tick of the watch, and the laboured breath of the sufferer, telling how life struggled in its prison.

The invalid moved uneasily on her pillow.

"Dear mamma!" said Ruth, whispering, for she knew not what to say.

"Lock the door," said Mrs. Raymond, with effort; "I must speak with you alone."

Ruth obeyed, and nestled by her mother's side.

"I must not conceal from you, my poor girl," said her mother, in slow and laboured accents, "that you are soon to lose me, perhaps this very night." (Ruth screamed with terror, but that gentle voice recalled her.) "My physician has told me this, and I am ready to go, ready to obey God's will in death as in life. But I must say a few words to you while my rea-

L 2

son is preserved to me. Prepare yourself, call up religion to your aid, for your trial is near. Ruth, my
blessed child," and here the sufferer's voice sank to a
whisper, " for the last few months my life has been one
of hypocrisy. My heart has been breaking beneath
smiles. Your father's character has undergone a
fearful change." (Here Ruth felt the bed shake with
the convulsive tremour of her dying mother.) " I have
no strength nor heart to tell you *how* this change has
operated; the whole aim of my existence has been to
conceal it. Ruth, your father *hates* me." (Here Ruth
recalled that look which had so terribly excited her.)
" At times he bends over me with *such* looks, and then
hour by hour I hear his sleepless footstep, tramp,
tramp, till it enters my very brain. Oh God, that it
should be so ! Oh God, that I who would die for him
should be his victim ! My faith, my hope is, that with
my death the balance of his character may be restored ; but should it not, it is for you, Ruth, to preserve
his reputation at all hazards. Swear to me" (and in
her excitement she rose up in bed, forgetful of her weakness), "swear to me that you will be to him as a child,
what I have been as a wife ; that you will conceal his
infirmities, and not breathe them to the winds. Ruth,"
she continued, almost wildly extending her emaciated
arm, and reeling to and fro, " swear."

Ruth knelt by the bedside as in a terrified dream,
but her voice became collected as she said,

" I will be to my father as a child, what you have
been to him as a wife, so help me God."

Mrs. Raymond sank on her pillow, and Ruth remained on her knees, burying her head in the bedclothes,
and striving to *think* amid her gushing tears. Sudden-

ly she perceived that no breath was to be heard; and, extending her hand to that of her mother, she felt it cold and rigid in her grasp. Was this death, *death?* With a wild and piercing cry she fell on the floor, and when the door was forced for admittance, was found insensible.

That is a dim, cold hour that familiarizes the young with death, the contrast with living things is so terribly vast. Ruth rose from the bed on which she had been laid, and walked resolutely to her mother's apartment. The bustle for the newly dead was over; friends and attendants moved with that light tread which jarred not the senseless form, their eyes turning, as they moved on the white shroud, as if they might disturb her repose. The face of the death-sleeper was calm, and her hands crossed quietly on her breast.

Poor Ruth! for eighteen years she had felt the pressure of those warm and tender hands; they had chafed her frosty, dimpled fingers in childhood; they had rested on her forehead in sickness; then there had been the richer clasp, when the younger heart had reached the sacred portal of filial sympathy, and hand lay in hand, because soul became endeared to soul. And she should feel that touch no more; the close coffin, the heavy earth, would hide her *mother.* It was a bitter thought; nature almost scorned the decree that should sever such a tie. Those lips *must* speak their wonted accents of love, those eyes *must* unclose to meet hers. Ruth laid her hand upon the brow, the lips. They were cold, cold; she knew that this *was* death, and her heart seemed breaking.

Her father wept, and tried to comfort her; she was still and tearless, and turned to him vacantly; the

children stood around her, claiming her as their mother now, and asked her to *cry*, because it would make
her feel better; but no tears came.   At length Clarendon arrived, and folded her in his arms beside that
death-couch.   *He* had loved that mother well; *he*
knew the truth, the fadeless beauty of her lovely mind.

"Let us weep together, my own Ruth," he said, as
he pressed her to his heart.   "I would that she had
been *my* mother; but she is sanctified in my memory
as such.   We will *never* forget her, dearest; we will
talk of her, and love the spirit that hovers near to bless
us.   Weep, weep, my beloved, but let *me* wipe away
your tears."

Then Ruth wept, but she could not be comforted.

CHAPTER XXIV.

Ruth and her Father.—The Burial.

RUTH lingered in her mother's apartment after Clarendon's departure. She could no longer arrange the
pillow on the cold, hard bedstead to which that dear
form was transferred, but she smoothed the shroud,
and pressed down the snowy eyelids, and parted the
hair, whose sprinklings of white showed the first footstep of age or anxiety. No fear possessed her, for
stronger emotions prevailed, and drove the common
shudderings at death away. It seemed to her that
while she could kiss her lips and press her hand, something of her mother remained to her.

Mr. Raymond sat in the parlour, soothing the lamen-
tations that broke in sudden bursts from the children.
He put Rosalie to bed himself with more than customary care, told her that her mamma was in heaven,
and that she must love her still ; and when Ruth went
below from her mournful duties in the apartment of
death, she found him with his head bent over a table,
and his face hidden by his hands. A gush of tenderness rushed over her afflicted heart, and softened the
memory of that fearful death-scene. Was it not,
thought she, the delirium of disease that had operated
on her mother's last moments ? It would almost seem
so ; and with rapid reasoning she resolved that it *was*
so ; and, going to her father, for she loved him fondly,
she knelt down, and entwined her arms around him.
He seemed agitated and subdued, returned her caresses,

and, speaking in the broken tones of grief, bade her a fond good-night, and retired to rest.

Ruth said her sobbing prayers, and crept shiveringly to bed beside the motherless Rosalie, whose quiet repose gave no token of her recent tears. She sought her little warm hand, and crushed it closely in her own, as if to feel its life; but she could not sleep. Tumultuous feelings worked at her heartstrings.

"It was a wild death-fancy of that blessed spirit," thought she. "Strange, that God should have given such a dreary exit to one whose whole joy was to bless others. I should have thought she would soar upward in a vision of love and joy. Oh, mother, mother," she ejaculated aloud, "I could have borne to see you go in peace to your eternal home, but in mental darkness, in despair! Oh God, it is too sad, too fearful!"

The clock on the stairway struck two, yet Ruth slept not; and suddenly she was startled by footsteps in the passage, and saw a gleam of light beneath her door, and heard the lock of her mother's room turn. Conscious that it could only be her father, her heart beat very wildly, and, raising herself from her pillow, she listened intently. No sound was heard but Rosalie's light breath. Ruth laid herself again on her pillow; her pulse grew more excited, her head throbbed with the excess of her sensations. "Yet why," she thought for a moment, "might not love have prompted this solitary nocturnal visit? What could or should keep a fond husband from the remains of one so lovely?"

But no reasoning soothed her, and suddenly that *look* rushed upon her memory. She started to her feet, threw her dressing-gown about her, opened the door softly, and stood by her mother's room. The door was ajar. Shrinking with almost a sense of intrusion, she drew back a moment, and would have retired, when an unnatural sound arrested her. It was not a groan, but a kind of prolonged hiss, that went tingling through her brain. Slowly, softly, with instinctive caution, she pushed open the door, her bare feet making no sound, and stood riveted, for there was her father, pale and ghastly, wrapped in a sheet like a shroud, holding a light in his extended hand close to the face of the corpse, now hissing and now chattering, as he perused its still lineaments.

Ruth had no longer power to stand. Crouching down, she gazed as if fascinated, when suddenly her father's ungracious antics ceased, his face became rigid, his form stood erect, and that fierce, fixed, strong look of *hate* was bent upon the dead. Ruth knew not how long it lasted; her own eyes seemed, by a kind of horrible sympathy, to open and glare upon him; her hands were clinched, her heart almost stopped its beating; but when the figure, for it seemed no kin to her, turned slowly to depart, she sprang to her feet, hurried with light but frantic steps to her room, and, covering herself in the bedclothes, shook in the tumult of an ague-fit.

" Speak to me, Rosalie, speak to me, or I shall die," she whispered in her agony.

The unconscious child put her arms about her, and sank off again to pleasant slumbers.

The gray dawn rose cold and slow, and a new agony came over her, in the thought that her father was a madman, and might have marred the corpse. She dressed herself rapidly and went to the death-room.

All was quiet; and as she unbolted a shutter, the dim light of dawn revealed the ghastly but undisturbed rest of death. Ruth felt a sensation of thankfulness, and, kneeling down, laid her fevered forehead against the cold breast that lent no responsive throbbing. Sunlight came, and lit up the features to a less fearful hue; and Ruth took her pillow, and, sitting down by the body, reposed her head there, for it ached sadly. Nature, overtasked, brought her repose, and she slept until awakened by little Rosalie's hand clasping her own.

There was a strange contrast to that bewildering night in the proprieties of the breakfast-table. Mr. Raymond's manners betrayed no peculiarity, except, perhaps, a heightened cheerfulness. Ruth spoke with difficulty; her tongue seemed parched when she attempted to address him.

" He is not *mad*," she thought, as she noted his attention to the children, his household cares, his preventive kindness to herself. " I could almost wish he were."

Clarendon's arm supported Ruth in the funeral procession, along the road where they first met, but she had no heart for the tender recollections of that scene. Her father led Rosalie, and she looked jealously and distrustfully upon his movements, her grief almost shrinking to a span before her fear. No look or word justified her alarm on the melancholy way; but, as they stood around the grave, and all eyes were bent to the lowering of the body, she turned hers to his, and saw again *that* look bent over the coffin, and heard a hiss, like wind amid the cordage of a vessel, through his compressed lips. Her strained and breaking powers gave way, and she fell in hysterical convulsions into Clarendon's arms.

No one, not even Clarendon, saw in this scene any-thing but the mastery of strong grief; that terrible foun-tain of mystery was sealed.

M

CHAPTER XXV.

The Raymond Fête.

RUTH, once the petted child of domestic love, the veriest butterfly on life's flowers, was now to be the self-sacrificing woman; *filial love* her trial and her inspiration. Sometimes she fancied a growing paleness and tenuity about her father's forehead, a variable flushing of the cheeks, and a dryness in the palms of the hands, that indicated disease; and then it occurred to her that medical advice might be necessary; but an almost superstitious reverence for her death-bed vow, and a dread that the intimacy of a physician might reveal her father's infirmities, deterred her from consulting one. It was, indeed, difficult for one so inexperienced to tell the boundary between wilful passion and a wilder hallucination.

Three months passed away; the grass sprang freshly on Mrs. Raymond's grave, and Clarendon began to urge his claims to a consummation of his happiness.

"You are not mine, Ruth," he urged, "until I can see you in our own home. I am jealous of your lavish love for others. You have too many cares; there is a hurry and agitation in your manners, occasionally, ill-suited to your age and temperament, and unlike the playful repose of former days. I will steal you away from this absorbing group. I want my *own* breakfast-table, and those dear fingers peeping out from beneath a white morning-dress, to pour out our coffee in *two* cups.

Besides, dearest," and his voice became lower, " I fear your father is growing weary of my encroaching visits."

Ruth turned very pale, but she rallied herself, and her sweet, confiding accents reassured him.

A few days after, Mr. Raymond said to Ruth, abruptly, " We live too *humdrum* a life here. You are growing pale and mopish. I intend to give a ball."

Ruth started. " A ball, *father !*" (She had given up the more endearing appellation of her childhood since *that* night.) " You must be jesting ;" and she looked mournfully at her sable dress, the tears coming to her eyes.

" By no means," said Mr. Raymond, rubbing his hands in great glee ; " and here comes the proof that I am not going to shut up my fair daughter any longer."

Ruth looked up, and saw several men approaching with boxes and crates. They were opened, and Mr. Raymond called her attention to lamps, mirrors, and other articles of rare value and elegance.

Ruth clasped her hands in silence, and the tears, no longer to be restrained, fell into her lap.

" Away to your room, girl !" muttered Mr. Raymond, through his shut teeth. Ruth obeyed without looking up. If she had—

Evening came, and brought Clarendon. It was in vain for Ruth to conceal her distress ; and, as composedly as possible, she told her lover of her father's announcement.

Clarendon's brow clouded. " We must resist this singular idea," he said, " if only for your father's reputation."

Mr. Raymond soon appeared, in high spirits.

He had been employed in writing cards of invitation in Ruth's name, and, going beyond the village, included many persons of distinction in the city to whom he was a stranger.

Clarendon and Ruth urged their objections with as much delicacy as possible ; but they seemed to fall back as if cast on ice, until Mr. Raymond, turning fiercely to Clarendon, exclaimed :

" It is not strange that *you*, sir, should wish to shut up Ruth as in a nunnery. Had more eyes fallen on her, she would not have been so lightly won."

" Father," exclaimed Ruth, her susceptible nature at length excited beyond control, " if you care not for *me*, at least reflect a moment on this desecration of the dead. Look at that face," and she pointed to her mother's picture, " which now gazes upon us as we dare to slight her memory before the world."

Mr. Raymond looked up at the picture. It was taken when he first brought his young bride to the shelter of his home, and her smile was one of light and joy. Ruth followed her father's eyes as they sought the portrait. What she then saw Clarendon knew not, but he heard a cry of terror, and caught her, not fainting, but trembling and powerless, as she sank at her father's feet.

From that day Ruth offered no obstacle to the fête, nor spoke of it to Clarendon, but gave herself up, a passive spectator, to the elegant and costly decorations that were multiplying around. She often sighed deeply, yet tried to check her sighs, and talked to Clarendon and the children in secret of her mother.

Clarendon looked on with bitterness, for already the city rang with speculations on the Raymond fête.

Ruth's name, hitherto unknown, was noised with exag-
gerated expressions of her beauty and accomplish-
ments, and an invitation to Miss Raymond's ball was
the envied object of the day.

"Ruth," said her father to her, as the fairy prepar-
ations rose with all the beauty that wealth and taste
could givè, "what shall be your dress for the ball?"

"I wish none but this, father," she said, tremulously
pointing to her mourning suit; but, seeing him look
angrily, she added, "I will arrange some flowers in
my hair, and that will look gayly enough."

"No, no," answered Mr. Raymond, with a thoughtful air: "I will bespeak your dress."

"As you please," was Ruth's reply; and she retired
to her own apartment to weep anew.

On the evening before the dreaded day, as she and
Clarendon were sitting together, with a cloud of anxiety on their usually serene faces, Mr. Raymond entered.

"Your dress has come, Ruth," he said, laughing.
"It is black, too;

> "Dark as was chaos."

"Sir," exclaimed Clarendon, interrupting him, as he
saw the convulsive agitation of Ruth's features at her
father's levity, "you trifle too far with your daughter's
feelings; as my affianced wife, I claim—"

Mr. Raymond darted a ferocious look—was it not
the look?—at Clarendon, hissed a curse between his
closed teeth, and left the room.

"Clarendon," said Ruth, starting up, and laying her
hand impressively upon his arm, "I *must* not thwart
my father's will. I have sworn to it, and I will keep
my word if it leads me to the grave."

Clarendon looked grieved and offended.

"Have I *no* claim, then?" he asked. "What was the value of the gift of your affections without your confidence? You are too tame, Miss Raymond. The city teems with idle speculations, until you are a by-word. I almost fear you love the miserable gewgaws that have changed this peaceful mansion into a show-house, since you have not had the resolution to stop this exhibition."

Clarendon's spirit had all along chafed in respectful silence, and now that he spoke it was in bitterness.

"Now am I indeed miserable," said, Ruth mournfully detaining him as he prepared to go. "While you gave me your confidence and respect, I had sunshine on my way; but now, now—Alfred Clarendon, you *must* give me your confidence. I know not how sorely I am to be tried, but I feel that nothing less than an overmastering love will make you bear with me. Have *faith* in me, I implore you. I am endeavouring before God to act rightly, but I have a dark path to walk; the more dark to me, because my soul loves the open day. But you *will* trust me through it all; you will not take away my sole help, next to God's, your love."

Clarendon knew not how to interpret this wild language; but he saw the imploring eyes that were turned to his; he felt the tears that dropped from them, and the pressure of the hand pledged to be his own. Not long was the struggle between his light resentment and his affection, and he renewed his vows to love the trembling girl eternally, through weal or wo.

The illuminated gardens already blazed with light on the following evening, and still Ruth sat in her mourning suit, detaining Rosalie by her side. Her heart was full of wo.

"Come, sister," said the child, "put on my beautiful frock. It is covered with flowers. It is prettier than this black one."

"But, Rosalie," said Ruth, "it is for mamma that we wear the black."

"Poor mamma loved flowers," said the little girl, evasively.

Ruth sighed heavily.

"I won't wear it, then, if it makes you sigh so," said Rosalie, putting her arms round Ruth's neck. "Let us wear mamma's black."

"Are you dressed, Ruth?" said Mr. Raymond, in a hurried voice, at the door.

"Come in, father, and help me dress Rosalie," said Ruth, cheerfully; and in a moment she was on her knees, fastening the gay suit of the pleased child; her own mourning strangely contrasted with the new attire.

Mr. Raymond looked gratified at the butterfly guise of his little girl, and led her away. Just then a strain from the band provided for the orchestra swept along the passage.

"Music for the sacrifice!" sighed Ruth, gloomily unfolding the dress of rich silk velvet selected by her father.

"It was kind to let it be *black*," she said, bitterly.

No light of gratified taste or vanity beamed from her eyes, as she stood in faultless proportions before her mirror, with the folds of her dress falling gracefully around her; but her beautiful eyes were cast upward in mental prayer, and her voice murmured, "Thou knowest, mother, that I love thee."

Again her father's footstep was at the door, and again she cheerfully bade him enter. He looked admiringly upon her, and, presenting her a box, bade her open it. It contained a set of costly pearls, and she stood in silence as he clasped them on her white neck and rounded arms, and twined them in her hair.

"She should be a princess," he said, exultingly, leading her to the drawing-room.

Clarendon was there alone. He started with a thrill of wonder and pride as the exquisite apparition stood before him; and Ruth, forgetting her sorrows in his intense admiration, blushed and was glad.

CHAPTER XXVI.

Clarendon Unhappy.—Ruth and her Pastor.—A Renewal of Vows.

THIS was no time for Ruth's sensibility to be awakened to mournful emotions.   The diffused glow of
the countless lamps, the exciting note of the finely har-
monized band, the constellation of female beauty and
fashion, and her introduction to statesmen, officers, and
authors, filled her imagination, dazzled her eyes, elevated the tone of her conversation and manners, and
carried her away from her own exclusive sorrows.
She might even have been lifted too far on this giddy
height, have been too much elated by the novelty and
brilliancy of the spectacle around her, had not the hurried motions of her father, perceptible only to herself,
awakened her to the necessity of self-possession ; and
it was this thought that gave a gentle dignity to her
deportment, exalting her beyond the inexperienced girl
to the considerate hostess.

One individual, however, in that sparkling group,
became grave and sad ; and in proportion as the light
barks around him rose and floated on the waves of
excitement, did Clarendon moor up his kindlier feelings and fall into the shade.   Who that has looked in
solitude on one lovely face, listened to a voice of tenderness and trust, seen the glad footseps of welcome,
and heard the parting sigh for him, *for him* alone, from
his own peculiar treasure, but feels rifled when that
treasure is exposed to the many ?   Again and again,

as he perceived the admiration that swelled in the atmosphere where Ruth moved, he thought of her father's taunt, "Had more eyes seen her, she would not have been so lightly won." Then Ruth was such an exquisite listener, that she was an involuntary flatterer. Ought she, he thought, to listen thus to others? Are strangers to share the look that has so long been mine alone? With what thoughtful interest her eyes are raised to the talker! Heavens! can *emotion* dictate the sudden fall of those fringed lids? But she is led away to the dance; a stranger touches her white fingers; see her foot beating time to the measure, and now she floats off like an air-touched cloud, floats away from me!

Among the invited guests that night was the clergyman of the village. Age still laid his hand gently on the old man, leaving his faculties free and his affections kind; and he had enough of the curiosity of human nature, mingled with his interest for the Raymonds, to carry him at an unwonted hour to their residence. But when the illuminated garden burst upon his sight, and the music rolled upon his ear, he shrank back half alarmed, until the thought that Ruth might meet him in some quiet corner led him on; and with slow steps and a faltering mind he entered the sitting-parlour, the only apartment, except Ruth's and the nursery, unchanged in the elaborate arrangement. Exhausted by his walk, he took possession of the rocking-chair, so long occupied by the former mistress of the mansion, and with his eyes raised to her likeness, dwelt in revery on many things, until aroused by the bounding footsteps of little Rosalie. The child paused as she saw him, and was soon on his knee.

"Do you like my new frock ?" she said, pointing out to him its embroidered flowers.

The old man was silent and serious.

"There, now !" exclaimed Rosalie, pouting, "that is like sister Ruth ! when papa brought it home, she cried, and said she loved mamma's black the best."

The old man kissed Rosalie, and smiled kindly. Slipping from his knee, she ran to the dancing hall to tell Ruth he was there.

A look at her venerable friend, as his eyes were up-raised to that beloved portrait, stirred up the dormant current of her feelings ; and, going towards him, she eagerly clasped his extended hand. He pressed hers tenderly, drew her closely towards him, and read her countenance with his undimmed eyes long and earnestly. Ruth stood unquestioning, unanswering ; her only motion a glance at her mother's picture, her only utterance a deep, deep sigh.

"Poor child," said the old man, pityingly, "I am sure that all is right *here*," and he laid his withered hand on her throbbing heart.

"God bless you for your kind judgment," said Ruth, sadly ; "all *is* right as yet between me and heaven."

The preluding strain of the dance, for which Ruth was engaged, sounded from the room above. She hesitated for a moment, then suddenly kneeling down by her pastor's side, whispered,

"Bless me before I go."

He bent over her, his gray locks falling amid her pearl-crowned hair as he murmured,

"*God's* blessing be on you, my dear child, a better gift than mine."

A brighter light than ever emanated from physical

charms shone around Ruth as she re-entered the dan-
cing-hall. Her form was erect, her step light, her
eyes beamed forth a tremulous lustre, and her whole
air was elevated, as if angel-guests had cheered her
on ; and if she spoke less, the glittering sensibility of
her face, and the softened tones of her voice, were
doubly eloquent.

Clarendon saw this change, and fancying that the
love of admiration had wrought it, turned away and
sighed bitterly.

" Oh why," he thought, " was I indulged in the long,
sweet dream that she was mine only ? Fool that I
was, to know so little of woman's heart as to think its
feathery sail would not bow before the breeze of novelty and fashion ! and yet, who am I, that I should
dare to appropriate the brightest of heaven's creatures
to myself ? She ought to be admired and prized.
Can the sun shine, and men not see the blaze ?"

Thus thinking, Clarendon walked towards the window to inhale the evening air, for he was oppressed.
Just then he felt a soft touch on his arm, and his name
uttered by the voice whose lightest tones could thrill
to his soul's depths. He turned, and his decision was
instantly made.

" Ruth," he said, rapidly, " will you escape from
these people, and go with me for five minutes through
the back path to the grotto ?"

She looked at him a moment earnestly, and then
quietly extricating herself from the crowd, soon found
him by her side. He was silent during the short
walk, but drew her arm through his, and held her hand
with a tenacious clasp. The stars looked forth bright
and conqueringly as they receded from the illuminated

paths, and the softened notes of the French horns came gracefully on the breeze. But sights and sounds were unnoted. On reaching the grotto, Clarendon released the hand he held, and, standing before Ruth, addressed her in a voice of forced composure.

" I find you to-night," he said, " suddenly transformed, a new creature. I sought and won your affections in solitude, before you knew your own power or the feebleness of my claims. Selfishly forgetting the demands of society, I never dreamed how gloriously my forest-flower would burst forth before the world; but now the illusion is dissolved. I find you by acclamation the idol of the crowd. I find you *fitted* for this new sphere by a natural grace, that raises you even above the forms of fashion; and, Ruth, pardon me, Ruth, but your sparkling eyes, your glowing cheeks, your airy footsteps, say that you *prize* this new-found, fairy land of existence. What, then, is my duty? I, who have appropriated your young affections perhaps too soon, too engrossingly? Here, on the very spot I sought them, I leave them free. No bitter taunt shall again tell me that you were ' lightly won.' I will not say how my heart will be riven by this sacrifice; how the world, where the star of your loveliness is to culminate, will be to me dark and cheerless. I will crush these selfish feelings, and bear my sentence like a man."

There was a very slight pause before Ruth replied; but, when her voice was heard, its truthfulness was worth a thousand oaths.

" I cannot *thank* you, Alfred," she said, " for releasing me from this voluntary bondage. The cage of your love is too bright and golden for me to wish to fly

N

away. And what if the world does look temptingly ?
So much the more thankful am I for this good, strong
arm" (and she entwined her own in his), " to hold me
amid its vanities. Alfred," she continued (and her
words, losing their playfulness, rose to a sweet solemnity), " here, on the spot where I gave you my first
affections, I renew the vow, and call upon *her* spirit,
who sanctioned me then, to witness from her angel-
home how dearly, how undividedly I love you."

It was enough ; and in expanding confidence they
retraced their footsteps to the house. Was the music changed ? Was the air more free ? Clarendon
thought so as he gave himself up to the full assurance
of requited faith.

" *Let* them love her ! *Let* them adore her ; she deserves it !" he thought, as, in rapt enthusiasm, he followed her with his eyes amid the throng ; " but she is
mine, mine only."

CHAPTER XXVII.

The Night succeeding the Ball.

THE half hour after a brilliant party is one of the most animated in the world, where a happy family gather together, to reveal each his own little experience, and to let fall the tribute of sympathy into the social hoard. But there is no sadder season to the careworn. The dying lamps, mocking the late universal blaze; the deep silence, succeeding to animated voices and thrilling music; the spoiled banquet, the broken wreaths, the laggard footsteps of the sleepy attendants, all join in melancholy resemblance to the soul's deserted festivals of hope and joy.

With half-shut eyes Ruth threw herself upon a *fauteuil* awaiting her father's good-night. Many hopes rushed up into the little space in which her reflections turned, from the past scene of fascinating enchantment to the present aspect of desolation. A quiet home with Clarendon was in her revery. She felt how grateful it would be to her fond heart, when his just taste could regulate her more enthusiastic mind, when his true affection could fill up the wants of his existence. "How superior he is to the many," she thought, as her fancy brought him before her in manly beauty and intellectual power! "Even among those reputed great and accomplished, I see but him!"

"I am glad he doubted me!" she exclaimed aloud, clasping her hands with girlish ardour. "If he had not, I could not have told him again how inexpressibly dear he is to me !"

She was recalled from her momentary ecstasy by seeing her father treading on tiptoe through the passage, as if searching for some concealed object. As he observed her, he put his finger on his lip in token of silence, and she saw in his face the terrible concentration of his fiercest passions. Approaching her softly, he asked in a low but wild tone,

"Have you seen him ? Have you seen him ?"

"Seen whom, father ?" asked Ruth.

"So, you are not in the plot," he said, looking hardly at her ; "but darker deeds than this have come to light. If you are *not* in the plot, I must forewarn you. Look here, child," he continued, coming close to her ear, "if a man (I don't say who) comes to your bedside with a dagger, take this gunpowder, and lay a train to my door. I'll fix him in five minutes. Holla, there !" he cried, as a fancied figure crossed his imagination, and with a wild spring he dashed at one of the windows.

An instantaneous, an almost preternatural calmness took possession of Ruth. Going towards him, she looked steadfastly in his face, and said resolutely, "Father, come here." He obeyed her without remonstrance, and she drew him by the hand to a seat beside her.

"Father," said she, "we have not talked over this gay ball yet ;" and she began to discuss cheerfully the events of the evening. It was very singular to perceive the ease and grace with which his thoughts reverted to more gentle themes ; and, when Ruth kissed him and retired to rest, he was as docile as a child.

But it was not thus with her. The struggle had been too violent to pass off without reaction. Shutting the door, she threw her arms above her head, clasped them wildly, trod her room hurriedly, and muttered, " Mad ! mad ! mad !" She strained her sight as if there were some object to blást her in the distance, and every sound seemed a dread summons to her affrighted ears.

After a while this nervous terror passed away, a cold perspiration stood on her forehead, and she be. came calm.

Her first regulated impulse, even at that late hour, was to go to the library and examine a medical book on the subject of insanity. It was a piteous spectacle to see the poor girl, still arrayed in the rich costume of the ballroom, conning over, in solitary misery, the stages of a father's mental derangement. Too surely were they traced there ; and, rising from her melan. choly task, pale but collected, she returned to her bed. room.

It was surprising to her at first to reflect on her mother's blindness to the real cause of her sorrow; but when she traced the gradual development of the dis. ease, and how, under the class denominated *malevolens,* it had wreaked its force in hatred to one individual, leaving the faculties free on every other subject, she was reconciled to this apparent ignorance.

But who would be the next object of this delirious hostility was now her thought, and she shuddered as it crossed her mind. Was she to tell Clarendon that she was in the power of a madman, and that madman her own father ? Then she remembered her singular command over him, when, despite of her terror that night, her instinctive resolution caused her to address him with a tone of authority. Then recalling her vow, it seemed to her that this very power was given her to shield him and keep his infirmities from the world.

"Nothing but heaven can guide me," she murmured to herself; "nothing but trust in God in this wild and dreary hour. Mother, look down upon me! Father of mercies, pity me, for I am most low, most wretched." Then, sinking on her knees, her heart, but not her lips, arose in prayer.

Rising more calm, she unfastened the pearls from her hair. It seemed an age since her father placed them there; so varied and deep had been the excitement of the last hours, such wild transitions from what the world calls joy and triumph to the heart's deep, unhoping wo. Who that saw her treading her hall like the genius of delight, could fancy her as she stood now, pale, stricken, comfortless? Sleep had settled on the world; eyes undeserving, perchance, of repose, were now calmly closed, and soft visions beguiling their rest, while she, the pure, the loving, the glad (when joy *could* smile), kept her vigil of alarm and grief.

But grief and alarm, wild and wakeful though they be, must yield to God's blessed nightly minister, and poor Ruth sank to sleep and forgot her woes. Yet her grief, though deep, was not permitted to be of long duration; she was awakened by the rattling of the lock of the door, and, opening her eyes, saw her father. He was wrapped in his dressing-gown, and held in one hand a light, and in the other a pistol. Advancing to the bedside, he leaned over her and whispered,

" I have seen him from my window; he is just under the shrubbery with a drawn dagger !"

" Who, father, for Heaven's sake, who ?" cried Ruth,
starting up.

" Alfred Clarendon," he shouted, with his wildest
look of hate ; " I warned you before."   Then springing to the window, he discharged his pistol into the
shrubbery, and Ruth sank on her pillow with a piercing cry.

CHAPTER XXVIII.

The Departure.

THE cry with which Ruth threw herself on her pillow was followed by such a gush of untempered misery as angels must almost weep to witness. Her father had suddenly retired, and though he pursued an imaginary victim, yet what might not even a few hours unfold of dreadful reality ? Rosalie still slept, the fatigue of the preceding night wrapping her in unwonted repose. Ruth pressed her cheek tenderly as the dawning light fell upon her innocent slumbers.

" Alas, alas !" thought the miserable girl, " what if this precious child be the next victim to her father's delirious vengence ? What can shield her helplessness from his insane strength ? Blessed mother, well was it that your gentle spirit fled early from this fearful strife ! Look down and shield this little one !"

The possibility of such a painful visitation from her father as that she had been contemplating, made the thought of him horrible to her imagination, coupling it with every association of disgust and dread. She strove to master her feelings, called up the filial piety of her nature, and strengthened it by the aid of reason ; but the idea of mere brute power levelled against the fragile and beautiful being so peculiarly thrown on her protection, chilled her habit of dutiful affection. Restless and wretched, she dressed herself, even at that early hour, and, *locking the door* on the little sleeper, went down stairs. The domestics were not yet risen,

and the few shutters her father had thrown open revealed the faded wreck of the luxurious yesterday.
It may seem singular that she felt no personal fear,
but there are many examples which justify this kind of
confidence in those intimately associated with the insane. Passing through the other apartments, she entered the common parlour, and saw her father. He
sat in her mother's rocking-chair, with his hands hanging listlessly by his side, and his whole attitude characterized by an overwhelming despondency; all the
daughter was roused within her; her harsher feelings
gave way, and the full tide of tenderness flowed anew.
She stood close beside him, and, gently putting her
hand on his head, drew it towards her, and bent her
lips to his forehead. He sighed heavily, but allowed
his head to lean against her bosom, and her arms to
enfold him.

" My dear father," said Ruth, "you seem very unhappy."

He looked up in her face and replied slowly,

" I am a murderer !"

The poor girl shuddered and trembled in every limb,
even while conscious of the illusion, but caressed him
more tenderly, for his melancholy tone and looks kept
alive her awakened sensibility. But, suddenly pushing
her away, he said,

" The officers of justice will be here in an hour.
We must have the start of them and be gone."

" Where are we to go ?" inquired the bewildered
Ruth.

He looked cunningly as he said, " We do not tell
our secrets to women; all your business is to be
ready."

"Delay *one* day only ; but *one* day, father," entreat‑ed Ruth.

"She would have me hung !" he muttered ; "I thought you loved me, Ruth," he continued, despond‑ingly.

"I do love you, father," she exclaimed, earnestly, taking his hand.

He brushed away the hair from her forehead, and looked at her kindly as he said,

"You will not betray your poor father, then; though the whole world forsake me, you will not ? You have been a good child since the first moment you lay help‑less in my arms ; but I tell you," and he put his mouth close to her ear with a shout, "*I killed him ! Now* will you not leave me to be hung ?"

"I will *never* betray or leave you, my dear father," said Ruth, soothingly; "but you must drive away these gloomy thoughts."

Mr. Raymond did not appear to listen to her.

"We shall have to ride by the gibbet," he muttered. "I have heard it creaking and clattering ever since— you know when. But quick, Ruth, quick," he urged, hurryingly, "if you would not see your father swing‑ing like a felon. They mean to wait for no forms ; blood for blood is the cry."

Ruth rushed to her apartment for a moment's thought. What could she do ? The rapidity of her father's resolution and movements allowed no pause ; her only hope was, that change of scene might have a salutary effect on his disease. Calling the housekeeper, she stated to her, as calmly as possible, that circumstan‑ces of importance made it necessary for her father to begin a journey immediately. She endeavoured to recollect every circumstance important to the comfort of the household, but not until it became impossible to delay longer could she speak of little Rosalie.

"You must not awake her," she said, trying to speak cheerfully, "until I am gone, and then tell her that I will send a doll and some books from the city." She dared not trust a look at the child.

Ruth's next movement was to write two letters. The first was the following, to her old pastor.

"*My respected Friend.*—A very pressing emergency calls my father from home, and he wishes me to accompany him. I am somewhat comforted in this sudden arrangement by the belief that you will interest yourself in our little group. Let me ask you to see them often, and to pray with *them* and for *me*.

"With affectionate respect,
"Your RUTH RAYMOND.

Over the next sheet Ruth paused a moment, pressed her hand anxiously to her forehead, looked upward as if for aid which earth could not give, and then, without faltering, wrote on :

"I have only a few moments to tell you, my best beloved, a sad, wild story that will rend your heart. My father is insane. He believes that he has murdered you, and that he is pursued by officers of justice. We leave home immediately, in what direction I know not, but will give you the earliest information. Your safety, thank Heaven, is secured by this determination. Keep from my father's presence at all hazards, and fear nothing for me. He regards me with the utmost ten-

derness, and I can control him in most things.   Perhaps
change of scene will benefit him.   If I had only time
to consult you or a physician—even good Dr. Gesner
is absent.   I must look up to heaven now, for earth
can scarcely aid me.   My father's movements seem
like a kind of fate, they are so imperative.

"Dear Alfred, my heart is very sad at the thought
of leaving you thus.   I can fancy all your surprise and
sorrow.   And *must* you have a sorrow that I may not
sooth?   *That* was to have been my privilege.   Is not
mine a most peculiar grief?   I must not dwell on it.
I will think of your love, and solace myself in its faith-
fulness.   I will recall the grotto scene, and live over
again in the memory.

"My little Rosalie is sleeping.   I dare not look at
her.   You will see her often; she will talk to you
of me.

"Dear, dear Alfred, beware how you follow me!   I
will not answer for your life a moment if you do.   I
have a fearful security now.   *He thinks you dead.*   Oh,
my beloved, what a desert would this world be to me
if that were true!   I must keep away tears from my
father's sight, so I will write no more lest they should
fall.   Your own   R. R."

As Ruth closed and sealed this letter, and gave it to
the housekeeper to be presented to Clarendon at his
evening visit, the reality of her departure was made
but too evident by the sound of trunks in the hall, and
the carriage drawing up to the door.

She looked despairingly from her window over the
beautiful landscape, on the hills and vales of her childhood, so calm in their morning brightness.   It was the

first time she had ever left her home ; it was her world. Oh how different from the wilderness on which she was about to be thrown! She looked to the distant trees that hid her mother's grave, to the garden where every walk, every blossom was hallowed by some tender association ; and then, with deeper emotion, turned to her own apartment, the shrine of her life's treasures. Rosalie still slept the unconscious, blessing sleep of childhood on the bed where Ruth's infantile repose had been shed, where her heart had beat to happiness, where her tears had been dried. She crushed down her spirit of wo, and with a stifled sigh closed the door on the slumbering child, without venturing to imprint a parting kiss on her cheek.

Her father appeared to have recovered his self-possession in the necessity of immediate exertion. His orders were clear, though hurried, and his pecuniary arrangements well regulated. The domestics gathered with wondering eyes about the passage, some with a significant expression of sadness. Mr. Raymond handed Ruth to the carriage, and took his seat beside her. Then, as the horses started, he rubbed his hands exultingly, and exclaimed,

" Safe, safe !"

The trial of *filial love* was consummated.

O

CHAPTER XXIX.

Clarendon's Visit to the Village.—A Letter.—An Interview.

CLARENDON left home for his accustomed evening
excursion, in one of those moods that belong only to
youth. His thoughts bounded from a happy past only
to revel in a blissful future ; poetry burst from his
lips, classical images clustered in his imagination, and
when he felt himself alone on the roadside that led to
the residence of his beloved, he leaped and sang aloud
in the mere buoyancy of his joy. Nature seemed in
sympathy with his happiness. The slanting sunbeams
gave a golden glory to the waving fields, the birds
trilled forth their vesper songs, and heaven smiled
throughout its azure depths.

As he entered the gate it swang to with the accustomed sound that was wont to summon Ruth to meet
him with her radiant welcome. He looked eagerly
towards the portico.

Not there ! Where was the waved handkerchief,
where the flowing garments, where the bright hair
tinged with the evening sunbeam, where the springing step, the extended hand, the loving smile ? He
trod the piazza with a lover's pang, opened the closed
door, and stole softly to the parlour to surprise and
chide the truant girl. It was deserted, and he rang
the bell. The housekeeper appeared with Ruth's letter, and, giving it with a silent courtesy, retired. He
tore it open, and his eyes ran wildly over the fearful

contents. What a revelation of misery! The floor seemed to fail beneath his feet, a deadly paleness overspread his countenance, he gasped for breath, and, thoroughly unmanned, fell panting into the nearest chair, beating his breast in the agony of suffocation. Deep was that heart-struggle, and it was not until he heard the sweet voice of Rosalie at his side that gentler nature conquered, and gave him relief in a burst of impassioned tears. The child climbed on his knees, threw her arms around his neck, and wept in sympathy.

Recovering from the first tumult of sorrow, a few mournful questions were asked and answered, and he was left alone, the light-hearted girl seeking gayer companionship. How every object around him spoke of his beloved! There was the book in which he had read to her ; the song he had last brought her lay by her guitar, while her open workbox, rifled of some of its useful prettinesses by her present wants, still retained many a little token of its owner's taste and industry. He took up the precious trifles, and pressed them to his lips and forehead ; and then a sudden sting of anguish shooting through his frame, he sprang up and rushed through the garden to the grotto. How still, how deathly still, was that sacred spot! His pulses were almost audible. Was this the place where she had so lately stood, living, glowing, loving? The same stream was flowing on, the same trees murmured in the breath of evening, the same flowers sent up their perfume on the breeze, but all was changed to him! His soul sickened, his knees trembled, he threw himself on the ground, and groaned aloud.

But Clarendon had cultivated a trust in Providence

amid life's sunshine, and now it came to him unsought amid its storms. A voice of mercy was heard whispering to his withered soul. Resisted at first by the fearful tempest of despair, it murmured again and again "peace, peace" in that dreary hour, and at length he bent before God in prayer.

A dreary week passed away, and he received the following letter from Ruth :

"I have purposely avoided writing, my own Alfred, lest you should follow me, and expose yourself to danger. Be comforted; my father is calm and happy. I am surprised at the resources of his mind, now that circumstances have thrown us into such intimate connexion. He is recalling the poetry of youth, and then he speaks with such tenderness of my blessed mother! Oh Alfred, will not this glorious temple of mind be restored to perfect symmetry? I have not yet mentioned your name to him, but in some calm and happy moment I will tell him that you live and love us still.

"Our movements are erratic, for he loves to linger where the beautiful and wild blend in natural scenery, and I am only too happy to aid his mental repose amid such favourable scenes. We shall visit Trenton and Niagara. I am almost jealous of this enjoyment apart from you. We, who have traversed together God's humbler natural walks with such sympathy, should go hand in hand to the mounts of his glory. But I encourage myself in this privation with the thought that I shall be better fitted for your companionship after this test of my fortitude and principles, than if I had glided from the retreats of a tranquil home to a life of love and repose with you; and why should *I* be entitled to heaven on earth, more than the myriads who have borne the cross of suffering and care before me? And would it not be heaven on earth to enjoy your love unembarrassed by the afflictions that surround me? My poor, poor father!

"Farewell; think of me in prayer,

"R. R."

Could anything have caused Ruth to forget the peculiar trials of her destiny, they would have been eradicated in the lofty and sublime associations excited by the magnificent scenery on the Kaatskill Mountains, the Pisgah which shows so fair a land of American promise; and, in truth, hope and courage did wait like ministering angels around her, and her filial love seemed meeting its reward in the springing lightness of her young bosom.

On one afternoon, those long, luxurious, balmy afternoons of a highland summer, Ruth and her father strolled far from the mountain house on the rugged and romantic road to the Kaatskill Falls, with which they had already become familiar; Mr. Raymond, from the restlessness of his mind, seeking novelties in the surrounding paths, and Ruth finding in natural scenery the best resource for the indulgence of her "thick-coming fancies." Wearied with their rambling excursion, they seated themselves on a rock to enjoy the gathering radiance about the setting sun, trusting to the moonlight and their knowledge of the road for their safe return. They sat in view of the Falls, the sound of its deep plunge swelling around, the wild and warm-toned light among the moving clouds glorifying the clear firmament, while mountain and ravine lay still as if meekly awaiting day's parting blessing. Fascinated by the scene, the father and daughter drank in the thousand revelations of nature as they burst from the changing heavens and the tinted earth, and sat until the large round moon trod calmly up the eastern sky.

A holy tenderness dilated Ruth's trusting heart as she turned her earnest face to its disk. Other objects around her had no immediate association with her lover; but the moon, the classic moon, how often had she raised her eyes towards that fair circle with him! Her father sat calmly by her, and placing her hand in his without waiting his bidding, she began a song dear to Clarendon. Her voice rose melodiously on the stillness, bearing her heart's harmony on every tone.

"Father," she said (for the time seemed fitting to her), "do you know who loves that song?"

"I love it, my darling," was his reply, and his hand gently pressed hers. "It suits well the pathos of your voice."

"Alfred Clarendon taught it to me," she said, falteringly.

Alas, poor Ruth! No sooner had that name escaped her lips, than a fierce, wild yell from her father pierced her ear, ringing and echoing from hill and depth; his eyes glared in the moonbeams, he tossed his arms furiously in the air, and, starting from her side, dashed away amid the gloom of a neighbouring thicket.

Ruth, with outspread hands, screamed wildly for his return, and was springing to follow him, when, suddenly, a form, closely enveloped in a cloak, stood beside her; her name was uttered in well-known accents, and she was pressed to Clarendon's heart. Concealing her hastily in the shade of the rock, he threw himself at her feet, with pleading eyes and clasped hands urging her to return with him.

"Come with me, Ruth," he said, "and let me protect you by the right which, in happier days, you promised to delegate to me. I swear to you," he urged, as he saw the mournful denial in her expressive face, "that I too will be a wanderer while you are in this peril. You would pity me if you knew the horrible fancies that attend me when I see you not; unless I watch at a distance the heavenly repose of your face, life grows a burden. Oh, let me then bathe my spirit in its unconscious sweetness; let me only hear your voice, and quench the thirst of my soul in its delicious melody, and I can live, and my dreams will be almost of heaven. Then come, dear, dear Ruth; escape while all is well; while this precious hand, warm with life and pulsation, rests thus within my own. Come to a tranquil home; where my arms can shield you, my love comfort you. Look on me, beloved, and say that you will be mine."

"I cannot leave my father," said Ruth, in a scarcely audible tone.

"You *must* leave him; it is your duty," said Clarendon, impetuously. "Is he not a madman? Who will guaranty that this delicate frame, trembling even by my side, shall be free from his violence? Heaven and earth! What shall I say to move you?" he exclaimed, pressing his forehead with his clasped hands. "Have pity on me! My heart is rent with love and terror. Where, gentle and blessed girl, should your shelter be but in my arms?"

Where indeed, thought Ruth; and she leaned her head like a trusting child against his bosom, and gave herself up to the overflowing tenderness of her agitated heart.

"You are, you will be mine own Ruth," he whispered, triumphantly. "You will repay nights and days, spent only in the thought of you, by your confiding love. I will be as a son to your father if he will receive my love; if not, there are asylums where—"

Ruth started from his arms, a look of intense and mournful indignation revealing her inmost feelings, and with repulsing hands thrust him from her. "God be thanked," she said, wildly, "for this cruel remembrance. I might, perchance, have faltered in my better purposes. Away, tempter! The only asylum for my father is near his child's breaking heart."

Then, as if fearing her harshness might too much wound the feelings of her lover, she turned to him mournfully, and took his drooping hand within her own.

Just then her father's voice was heard as he issued from the thicket, chiming a careless song, and then he called her name.

One long, earnest embrace, as if death were to ensue, was given by that wretched pair; then Ruth tore herself away, and Clarendon, wrapped closely in his cloak, followed them cautiously through the wild pathway to the hotel.

CHAPTER XXX.

Trenton Falls.

MR. RAYMOND grasped Ruth's arm with unconscious roughness, and hurried her on, now looking about with a wild air of expectation, and then laughing with a childish vacancy. As the full moonlight shone on his features, his anxious child saw a change from their recent expression of tender regard, to the hard, cold tone which had characterized them in his period of excitement. They were not yet marked by *hate;* thank God, he loved *her* still; but the maniac began to be developed more distinctly; and when she saw that, as a tear dropped on his hand from her eyes, he held it up to the moonbeams, and laughed, and cried "Hurra!" she knew that sympathy was gone. She felt that she stood beneath a lava mountain, heaving to its explosion; but the Christian habit of her mind referred all things to a presiding Deity; and when her eyes had turned upward a moment, and her lips moved in almost involuntary prayer, her fluttering heart grew calm. Something of joy, too, played over her troubled spirit, at the idea of Clarendon's vicinity; it seemed as if another Providence was watching over her. And what felt that covert wanderer, as he saw the flutter of her garments, and remembered the pressure of her trembling form? The moonlight glory was no longer sought for inspiration; the mountains uplifted their noble heights unheeded, for the fair vision of his heart was before him, in her youth and loveliness.

And now Ruth and her father are once more on their bright and beautiful Hudson, while the boat treads her way like an untried courser. He was comparatively calm, and nature, like a sweet restorer, healed her wounded heart. The blue, massy hills, as they heaved heavenward, lent her a kinder strength and engendered a lofty repose; a trust that He who created and ruled the universe would guard over her, and thus she became calm as a part of that great and exquisite whole.

The deportment of Clarendon was of the most cautious and delicate character; though invisible, he contrived to spread an atmosphere of tenderness around her. Books were laid on the table with marked passages, or flowers that she best loved; and sometimes a deep, full sigh, and a whispered name, when none were near, told the story of watchful affection. Dear and romantic was the charm of this intercourse, lending a precious interest to existence, and calming the tumult of her filial cares.

At length they arrived at Trenton Falls, that glorious handiwork of triumphant nature. With what innocent yearnings did Ruth sigh for Clarendon to lead her steps to this sublime revelation of the Omnipotent! As she sat musing in the parlour of the hotel, her father entered hurriedly, and one look revealed to her that he must have seen her lover.

As he stood before her with shut teeth, glaring eyes, and rigid form, she rose and clasped her hands imploringly, forgetting, in the horror of the moment, to use the slight authority which she yet held over him. He said nothing, but drew her arm within his own, and almost dragged her through the woods to the steep stairway which descends to the bottom of the ravine. The sky was ominous with flitting clouds, and the gushing waters looked sternly beneath the scowling heavens. An undefined dread crept over Ruth as she saw the narrow ledge on which she was to tread, where the rolling stream dashed to her very footsteps, and the jutting rocks soared up on either side, as if to shut a death-cry from the world. In such a spot, love should lead with fond and careful tread, soothing the over-wrought heart with tones of tenderness; but poor Ruth's arm was grasped by a maniac; one step, and the whirling abyss would close on her for ever. Her father released her a moment, and stood sternly contemplating the grandeur of the spectacle; at length he spoke, and his words grew eloquent.

"Ruth," he said, solemnly, "seems it not as if unseen spirits haunted these cliffs? It would be a noble place to die. No need for man to raise monuments here. Let others go to the groves, and gardens, and streams, where the rose blushes, and the lily pales, and rainbows rest, and skies throw out their western glow, and seashells whisper; where woodland melody resounds, and the clear stars glisten, and the moonlight floats in joy; let others sleep, if they will, beneath chiselled marble wet by human tears, but give me a grave like this, amid clouds and gloom, where the veil is rent from stormy nature, and let my requiem be these cataract voices. Take me, take me," he muttered softly, as if appealing to some distant object; and then waving his arms in passionate gestures, he stopped with a wild hurra, that rolled by the cliffs, and came back in fearful echoes.

Clarendon, protected by the dense foliage above,

had been an unseen spectator of this phrensy. With clinched hands and firmly braced feet, he stood prepared for some frightful catastrophe ; and when that echoed hurra reached him, and he saw Mr. Raymond about to carry Ruth onward by the passes below, unable longer to contain his feelings, he bounded down the steps like a maddened wolf. Had the rocks around him lifted their giant heads and cried forbear, his impulse would have prevailed. With an almost phrensied voice he cried,

" Ruth, Ruth, I adjure you, by the God of Heaven, not to peril your life with a madman."

Fatal precipitance ! Mr. Raymond, without reply, caught his helpless child in his arms, and, as if but a feather's weight lay there, leaped along the slippery way. He passed the frowning rocks, where trees rooted in the fissures seemed reeling to their fall, sprang the awful projections where the bounding waves dashed the dress of his trembling burden, and paused not even on the brink of those frightful steeps where the resistless torrent ran in its terrible strength below. Clarendon too pressed on, heedless of every obstacle, reckless of but one thought, to save the beloved of his heart. Once Ruth opened her eyes, and though unappalled by the threatening rocks, or the whirling waters, she met her father's gaze in its fixed and angry glare, and closed them again with sick and dizzy terror.

They had nearly reached that fatal spot, sacred to sad memories, where a plighted bride and a child fresh in the budding promise of life met each their tragic doom, when Mr. Raymond heard his pursuer close upon his steps. On he sprang more impetuously. He looked back; nearer, closer. Again he looked, and glared with his maniac eyes. Clarendon's outspread arms were near him, and he heard his desperate cry,

" Ruth, my bride, my affianced one, I will die with you or save you."

The madman laughed tauntingly, and his wild hurra echoed again from cliff to cliff ere he bounded over that fearful point. One spring, and the father and daughter sank where the whirlpool sends across its bubbling foam. Clarendon threw his length along the edge of the slimy rock, with his head over the waters, and braced his feet against a projecting point within his reach. Oh the intense, the life-long agony of that instant of time, before Ruth's garments were seen above the torrent. He clutched at them as with a death-grasp, but the maniac father struggled for his prize. Awful was the contest; twice he rose with his blasting look of hate full on Clarendon, then sank, and the gurgling waters closed over him for ever.

" God receive him to his peace," murmured Clarendon, as he drew, with an effort inspired by despair, the insensible form of his beloved to his arms. He carried her to a broader shelf of the rock, where the dashing spray pursued them more faintly; then wringing the water from her hair and wrapping her in his cloak, he called her by every endearing name to awake to life and love. He had never seen her cheek untinged by the hue of health, never touched her hand but its soft warmth had spoken of life; now that cheek was pale as the foam that quivered over her father's corpse; her hand lay motionless and cold within his own; and that hair too, that shining hair, the simplest twine of which was like threads of gold to him, strew-

P

ed the bare rock in its luxuriance. He chafed her
hands, and laid his cheek to bers, and felt for the beating of the heart so late responding to his own. Sensation slowly returned, and without unclosing her eyes
she whispered " father." Clarendon gently pressed
her hand and laid his lips to her damp forehead in silence.

"I will never desert you, father," said the half unconscious girl. "If I love Alfred Clarendon, I can
still be faithful to you. I have sworn it to my blessed
mother."

As she spoke large tears rolled from beneath her
closed lids. Clarendon essayed to speak, but he felt
choked. The unformed words died gaspingly away,
and he covered his face in unutterable emotion. Gradually her eyes unclosed; at first the cold high cliffs
and dashing torrent alarmed her; then she saw Clarendon, and a bright, warm blush of joy rushed over her
face like sudden sunbeams on snow. Then a deeper
consciousness followed, as he pressed her fondly to his
heart, and she attempted to rise from his arms; but,
embarrassed by a feeling of her weakness, she sank
back helplessly, and a sudden shade crossing her countenance, exclaimed,

"My father?"

"I could not save you both, dearest," said Clarendon, in a low tone, bending over her with deep emotion, and pointing mournfully to the cataract as it
came foaming by where the lost victim fell.

A strong hysteric cry burst from the unhappy girl,
and, forgetting her weakness, she sprang to her feet,
and stretched out her arms to the rushing streams as
if they could give back the lost, the dead.

" God knows how willingly I would have given my life for his," said Clarendon ; " a life valueless to me if you are not happy." And, as he spake, he knelt on the rock beside her, and bowed his head in his hands.

" My poor father," said Ruth, wildly, unheeding her lover's prostrate sorrow, " you sleep beneath the monuments you asked. The tears of love can never, indeed, fall on your grave."

Clarendon gently forced her from the scene. She leaned upon his arm as he guided her feeble steps along the dangerous way, and her piteous moans touched his inmost soul. At length, seeming to recall the ties that bound them, and resisting the selfishness of her grief, she bent her cold cheek to his hands and burst into tears.

" Do not think me ungrateful for the life you have preserved," she said, in sobbing accents. " Do not think that I love you less when I weep for my fa-ther."

" My poor, suffering Ruth !" said Clarendon, sooth-ing her like a child, but addressing her as a noble-minded woman, " in this wild scene and at this fear-ful hour, while I claim you mine, I seek no present token of tenderness from your shattered affections. I have traced the self-sacrificing *progress* of your heart's *love* through life's varied duties, and I know that the tender *daughter* will be the faithful *wife*."

Then Ruth yielded herself silently, in mournful confidence, to his guidance, and the first smile, when love and hope triumphed over tears, was for him.

THE END.

VALUABLE STANDARD WORKS

PUBLISHED BY

HARPER & BROTHERS, NEW-YORK.

HISTORY.

INSTITUTES OF ECCLESI-ASTICAL HISTORY, Ancient and Modern, in four Books, much Corrected, Enlarged, and Improved, from the Primary Authorities, by JOHN LAWRENCE VON MOSHEIM, D.D., Chancellor of the University of Gottingen. A new and literal Translation from the original Latin, with copious additional Notes, original and selected. By JAMES MURDOCK, D.D. 3 vols. 8vo.

THE HISTORY OF MODERN EUROPE: with a View of the Progress of Society, from the Rise of the Modern Kingdoms to the Peace of Paris, in 1763. By WILLIAM RUSSELL, LL.D.: and a Continuation of the History to the present Time, by WILLIAM JONES, Esq. With annotations by an American. 3 vols. 8vo. With Engravings, &c.

THE HISTORICAL WORKS OF WILLIAM ROBERTSON, D.D. 3 vols. 8vo. With Maps, Engravings, &c.

THE HISTORY OF THE DISCOVERY AND SETTLEMENT OF AMERICA. By WILLIAM ROBERTSON, D.D. With an Account of his Life and Writings. To which are added, Questions for the Examination of Students. By JOHN FROST, A.M. 8vo. With a Portrait and Engravings.

THE HISTORY OF THE REIGN OF THE EMPEROR CHARLES V.; with a View of the Progress of Society in Europe, from the Subversion of the Roman Empire to the Beginning of the Sixteenth Century. By WILLIAM ROBERTSON, D D. To which are added, Questions for the Examination of Students. By JOHN FROST, A.M. 8vo. With Engravings.

THE HISTORY OF SCOTLAND, during the Reigns of Queen Mary and of King James VI., till Accession to the Crown of Engla With a Review of the Scottish H tory previous to that Period. Inc ding the HISTORY OF INDIA. 8v

THE HISTORY OF THE D CLINE AND FALL OF THE R MAN EMPIRE. By EDWA GIBBON, Esq. With Notes, by t Rev. H. H. MILMAN. 4 vols. 8 With Maps and Engravings.

VIEW OF THE STATE OF E ROPE DURING THE MIDD AGES. By HENRY HALLAM. 8 From the Sixth London Edition.

INTRODUCTION TO THE LI ERARY HISTORY OF EUROP during the 15th, 16th, 17th, and 18 Centuries. By HENRY HALLA [In press.]

THE ANCIENT HISTORY THE EGYPTIANS, CARTH GINIANS, ASSYRIANS, BAB LONIANS, MEDES AND PE SIANS, GRECIANS, AND MAC DONIANS; including the Histo of the Arts and Sciences of t Ancients. By CHARLES ROLLI With a Life of the Author, by JAM BELL. First complete Americ Edition. 8vo. Embellished wi nine Engravings, including thr Maps.

PRIDEAUX'S CONNEXION or, the Old and New Testamen connected, in the History of t Jews and neighbouring Nations, fro the Declension of the Kingdoms Israel and Judah to the Time Christ. By HUMPHREY PRIDEAU D.D. New Edition. 2 vols. 8v With Maps and Engravings.

THE HISTORY OF THE AME ICAN THEATRE. By WILLIA DUNLAP. 8vo.

HISTORY OF THE REFORM ED RELIGION IN FRANCE. B the Rev. E. SMEDLEY. 3 vols. 18m

A HISTORY OF THE CHURCH, from the earliest Ages to the Reformation. By the Rev. GEORGE WADDINGTON, M.A. 8vo.

ANNALS OF TRYON COUNTY; or, the Border Warfare of New-York during the Revolution. By W. W. CAMPBELL. 8vo.

A NARRATIVE OF EVENTS CONNECTED WITH THE RISE AND PROGRESS OF THE PROTESTANT EPISCOPAL CHURCH IN VIRGINIA. To which is added an Appendix, containing the Journals of the Conventions in Virginia from the Commencement to the present Time. By F. L. HAWKS. 8vo.

HISTORY OF PRIESTCRAFT in all Ages and Countries. By WILLIAM HOWITT. 12mo.

THE CONDITION OF GREECE. By Col. J. P. MILLER. 12mo.

FULL ANNALS OF THE REVOLUTION IN FRANCE, 1830. To which is added, a particular Account of the Celebration of said Revolution in the City of New-York, on the 25th November, 1830. By MYER MOSES. 12mo.

THE HISTORY OF THE JEWS. From the earliest Period to the present Time. By the Rev. H. H. MILMAN. 3 vols. 18mo. With Engravings, Maps, &c.

HISTORY OF THE BIBLE By the Rev. G. R. GLEIG. 2 vols. 18mo. With a Map.

HISTORY OF CHIVALRY AND THE CRUSADES. By G. P. R. JAMES. 18mo. Engravings.

A VIEW OF ANCIENT AND MODERN EGYPT. With an Outline of its Natural History. By the Rev. M. RUSSELL, LL.D. 18mo Engravings.

SACRED HISTORY OF THE WORLD, as displayed in the Creation and subsequent Events to the Deluge. Attempted to be philosophically considered in a Series of Letters to a Son. By SHARON TURNER, F.S.A. 3 vols. 18mo.

PALESTINE; OR, THE HOLY LAND. From the earliest Period to the present Time. By the Rev. M. RUSSELL, LL.D. 18mo. Engravings.

HISTORY OF POLAND. From the earliest Period to the present Time. By JAMES FLETCHER, Esq. 18mo. With a Portrait.

SKETCHES FROM VENETIAN HISTORY. By the Rev. E. SMEDLEY, M.A. 2 vols. 18mo. Engravings.

HISTORICAL AND DESCRIPTIVE ACCOUNT OF BRITISH INDIA. From the most remote Period to the present Time. Including a Narrative of the Early Portuguese and English Voyages, the Revolutions in the Mogul Empire, and the Origin, Progress, and Establishment of the British Power; with Illustrations of the Botany, Zoology, Climate, Geology, Mineralogy. By HUGH MURRAY, Esq, JAMES WILSON, Esq., R. K. GREVILLE, LL.D., WHITELAW AINSLIE, M.D., WILLIAM RHIND, Esq., Professor JAMESON, Professor WALLACE, and Captain CLARENCE DALRIMPLE. 3 vols. 18mo. Engravings.

HISTORY OF IRELAND. From the Anglo-Norman Invasion till the Union of the Country with Great Britain. By W. C. TAYLOR, Esq With Additions, by WILLIAM SAMPSON, Esq. 2 vols. 18mo. With Engravings.

THE HISTORY OF ARABIA, Ancient and Modern. Containing a Description of the Country—An account of its Inhabitants, Antiquities, Political Condition, and early Commerce—The Life and Religion of Mohammed—The Conquests, Arts, and Literature of the Saracens—The Caliphs of Damascus, Bagdad, Africa, and Spain—The Government and Religious Ceremonies of the Modern Arabs—Origin and Suppression of the Wahabees—The Institutions, Character, Manners, and Customs of the Bedouins; and a Comprehensive View of its Natural History. By ANDREW CRICHTON. 18mo. Engravings, &c.

HISTORY AND PRESENT CONDITION OF THE BARBARY STATES. Comprehending a View of their Civil Institutions, Arts, Religion, Literature, Commerce, Agriculture, and Natural Productions. By the Rev. M. RUSSELL, LL.D. 18mo. With Engravings.

HISTORY of SCOTLAND. By Sir Walter Scott, Bart. 2 vols. 12mo.

"A beautiful illustration of the grace and effect which sober reality assumes when treated by the pencil of genius. In no work with which we are acquainted is the progress of manners painted with more historic fidelity, or with half so much vividness of colouring. This, the great charm of the work, will ensure it a lasting popularity." — Gentleman's Magazine.

"We have read this book with pleasure. The author throws over the events of the past that splendid colouring which gives charms to truth without altering its features." — British Critic.

"Sir Walter tells his story with infinite spirit, and touches his details with a master's hand." — Eclectic Review.

HISTORY of FRANCE. By E. E. Crowe, Esq. 3 vols. 12mo.

"The best English manual of French History that we are acquainted with." — Eclectic Review.

"The style is concise and clear; and events are summed up with vigour and originality." — Literary Gazette.

"A valuable epitome of French History: the author's impartiality and temper are highly commendable." — Asiatic Journal.

HISTORY of THE NETHERLANDS to the Revolution of 1830. By T. C. Grattan, Esq. 12mo.

"We have seldom perused a volume of history more pregnant with interesting matter, or more enlivened by a style combining vigour, ease, and sobriety." — Gentleman's Magazine.

"A compressed, but clear and impartial narrative." — Literary Gazette.

HISTORY of ENGLAND to the Seventeenth Century. By Sir James Mackintosh. 3 vols. 12mo.

"Contains more thought and more lessons of wisdom than any other history with which we are acquainted. The most candid, the most judicious, and the most pregnant with thought, and moral and political wisdom, of any in which our domestic story has ever yet been recorded." Edinburgh Review.

"His comments and elucidatio are admirable, throwing a power and striking light, both on the strea and on the conspicuous points English history" — Eclectic Review

"We would place this work in t hands of a young man entering pu lic life, as the most valuable and e lightened of commentaries on o English constitution." * * * " model of history." * * * "So mu of profound observation, of acu analysis, of new and excellent c servation." * * * "Of great valu and should be in the hand of eve investigating reader of history." Literary Gazette.

HISTORY of SPAIN and PO TUGAL. By S. A. Dunham, LL. 5 vols. 12mo.

"The very best work on the su ject with which we are acquainte either foreign or English." — At næum.

"A work of singular acutene and information." — Prescott's Histo of Ferdinand and Isabella.

HISTORY of SWITZE LAND. Edited by the Rev. D nysius Lardner, LL.D. 12mo.

"A very good and clear history a remarkable country and peopl — Leeds Mercury.

"Historical facts are candidly a fairly stated; and the author displa throughout a calm and philosophic spirit." — Monthly Magazine.

"We cannot quit the volume wit out commending it for the spirit truth and fairness which is eve where visible." — Athenæum.

HISTORY of THE ITALIA REPUBLICS. By J. C. L. Sismondi. 12mo.

"We warmly recommend th book to all who read history with eye to instruction. We have m with no recent historical work whi is written in so excellent a spirit." Scotsman.

"The struggles of Italy for fre dom, the glories she acquired, a her subsequent misfortunes, are po erfully sketched in this work." Gentleman's Magazine.

HISTORICAL AND DESCRIPTIVE ACCOUNT OF PERSIA. From the earliest Period to the present Time. With a detailed View of its Resources, Government, Population, Natural History, and the Character of its Inhabitants, particularly of the Wandering Tribes; including a Description of Afghanistan. By JAMES B. FRASER, Esq. 18mo. With a Map, &c.

HISTORICAL VIEW OF THE PROGRESS OF DISCOVERY ON THE NORTHERN COASTS OF NORTH AMERICA. From the earliest Period to the present Time. By P. F. TYTLER, Esq. With Descriptive Sketches of the Natural History of the North American Regions. By Professor WILSON. 18mo. With a Map, &c.

NUBIA AND ABYSSINIA. Comprehending the Civil History, Antiquities, Arts, Religion, Literature, and Natural History. By the Rev. M. RUSSELL, LL.D. 18mo. With a Map and Engravings.

A COMPENDIOUS HISTORY OF ITALY. Translated from the original Italian. By NATHANIEL GREENE. 18mo.

THE CHINESE. A general Description of the Empire of China and its Inhabitants. By JOHN FRANCIS DAVIS, F.R.S. 2 vols. 18mo. With Engravings.

AN HISTORICAL ACCOUNT OF THE CIRCUMNAVIGATION OF THE GLOBE, and of the Progress of Discovery in the Pacific Ocean, from the Voyage of Magellan to the Death of Cook. 18mo. With numerous Engravings.

UNIVERSAL HISTORY, from the Creation of the World to the Decease of George III, 1820. By the Hon. ALEXANDER FRASER TYTLER and Rev. E. NARES, D.D. Edited by an American. 6 vols. 18mo.

SALLUST. Translated by WILLIAM ROSE, M.A. With Improvements. 18mo.

CÆSAR. Translated by WILLIAM DUNCAN. 2 vols. 18mo. With a Portrait.

THUCYDIDES. Translated by WILLIAM SMITH, A.M. 2 vols. 18mo. With a Portrait.

XENOPHON. (ANABASIS, translated by EDWARD SPELMAN, Esq. CYROPÆDIA, by the Hon. M. A COOPER) 2 vols. 18mo. With Portrait.

LIVY. Translated by GEORG BAKER, A.M. 5 vols. 18mo. Wit a Portrait.

HERODOTUS. Translated b the Rev. WILLIAM BELOE. 3 vol 18mo. With a Portrait.

ATHENS: ITS RISE AN FALL: with Views of the Literature, Philosophy, and Social Life the Athenian People. By Sir LY TON BULWER, M.P., M.A. 2 vol 12mo.

A HISTORY OF NEW-YORK By WILLIAM DUNLAP. 2 vols. 18m Engravings.

THE HISTORY OF GREECE By Dr. GOLDSMITH. Edited by th Author of "American Popular Les sons." 18mo.

THE HISTORY OF ROME. B Dr. GOLDSMITH. Edited by H. HERBERT, Esq. 18mo.

A HISTORY OF THE UNITE STATES. By the Hon. S. HAL 2 vols. 18mo.

AN HISTORICAL AND DE SCRIPTIVE ACCOUNT o BRITISH AMERICA; compre hending Canada, Upper and Lowe Nova Scotia, New-Brunswick, New foundland, Prince Edward Island the Bermudas, and the Fur Coun tries: their History from the earl est Settlement; their Statistics, T pography, Commerce, Fisherie &c.; and their Social and Politica Condition; as also an Account of th Manners and present State of th Aboriginal Tribes. By HUGH MUF RAY, F.R.S.E. 2 vols. 18mo.

THE HISTORY OF ENGLAN By THOMAS KEIGHTLEY. 4 vol 18mo.

HISTORY OF THE EXPED TION TO RUSSIA undertaken b the Emperor Napoleon. By Ger eral Count PHILIP DE SEGUR. vols. 18mo.

HISTORY OF THE FINE ART viz.: Architecture, Sculpture, Pain ing, Engraving, &c. By B. J. Lo SING, Esq. 18mo.

TALES from HISTORY. By AGNES STRICKLAND. 2 vols. 18mo.

TALES from AMERICAN HISTORY. By the Author of "American Popular Lessons." 3 vols. 18mo. With Engravings.

UNCLE PHILIP'S CONVER-SATIONS with THE CHILDREN ABOUT THE HISTORY of VIRGINIA. 18mo. With Engravings.

UNCLE PHILIP'S CONVER-SATIONS with THE CHILDREN ABOUT THE HISTORY of NEW-YORK. 2 vols. 18mo. Engravings.

TALES of THE AMERIC REVOLUTION. By B. B. THAT ER, Esq. 18mo. Engravings.

UNCLE PHILIP'S CONVE SATIONS with THE CHILDRI ABOUT THE HISTORY of MA SACHUSETTS. 2 vols. 18 Engravings.

UNCLE PHILIP'S CONVE SATIONS with THE CHILDRI ABOUT THE HISTORY of NE HAMPSHIRE. 2 vols. 18mo. E gravings.

BIOGRAPHY.

PLUTARCH'S LIVES. Translated from the original Greek, with Notes, critical and historical, and a Life of Plutarch. By JOHN LANG-HORNE, D.D., and WILLIAM LANG-HORNE, A.M. A new Edition, carefully revised and corrected. 8vo. With Plates.

MEMOIRS of THE LIFE AND CORRESPONDENCE of MRS. HANNAH MORE. By WILLIAM ROBERTS, Esq. 2 vols. 12mo. Portrait.

THE LIFE AND DEATH of LORD EDWARD FITZGER-ALD. By THOMAS MOORE. 2 vols. 12mo.

MEMOIRS of AARON BURR. With Miscellaneous Selections from his Correspondence. By MATTHEW L DAVIS. 2 vols. 8vo. With Portraits.

TRAITS of THE TEA-PARTY; being a MEMOIR of GEORGE R. T. HEWES, one of the last of its Survivers. With a History of that Transaction; Reminiscences of the Massacre and the Siege, and other Stories of Old Times. By a Bostonian. 18mo. With a Portrait.

WONDERFUL CHARAC-TERS; comprising Memoirs and Anecdotes of the most Remarkable Persons of every Age and Nation. By HENRY WILSON. 8vo. Engravings.

THE LIFE of JOHN JAY; with Selections from his Correspondence and Miscellaneous Papers. By I Son, WILLIAM JAY. 2 vols. 8v With a Portrait.

A MEMOIR of THE LIFE WILLIAM LIVINGSTON, Mei ber of Congress in 1774, 1775, a 1776; Delegate to the Federal Co vention in 1787, and Governor of tl State of New-Jersey from 1776 1790. With Extracts from his Co respondence, and Notices of vario Members of his Family. By SEDGWICK, Jun. 8vo. Portrait.

RECORDS of MY LIFE. JOHN TAYLOR, Author of "Monsie Tonson." 8vo.

MEMOIRS of THE DUCHES D'ABRANTES (MADAME JUNOT 8vo. With a Portrait.

MEMOIRS of LUCIEN BON PARTE (Prince of Canino). 12m

THE LIFE AND REMAINS EDWARD DANIEL CLARK By the Rev. WILLIAM OTTER, A.M F.L.S. 8vo.

THE HISTORY of VIRGIL STEWART, and his Adventures capturing and exposing the Gre "Western Land Pirate" and h Gang, in Connexion with the Ev dence; also of the Trials, Confe sions, and Execution of a Number Murrell's Associates in the State Mississippi during the Summer 1835, and the Execution of five Pr fessional Gamblers by the Citizer of Vicksburg, on the 6th of July, 183 Compiled by H. R. HOWARD. 12m

PLUTARCH'S LIVES. Translated from the original Greek; with Notes, critical and historical, and a Life of Plutarch. By JOHN LANGHORNE, D.D., and WILLIAM LANGHORNE, A.M. New Edition. 4 vols. large 12mo.

LETTERS AND JOURNALS OF LORD BYRON. With Notices of his Life. By THOMAS MOORE, Esq. 2 vols. 8vo. With a Portrait.

THE PRIVATE JOURNAL OF AARON BURR, during his Residence in Europe, with Selections from his Correspondence. Edited by M. L. DAVIS. 2 vols. 8vo.

SKETCHES OF THE LIFE AND CHARACTER OF THE REV. LEMUEL HAYNES, A.M. By TIMOTHY MATHER COOLEY, D.D. With some Introductory Remarks, by WILLIAM B. SPRAGUE, D.D. 12mo. With a Portrait.

LIFE OF EDMUND KEAN. By BARRY CORNWALL. 12mo.

LIFE OF MRS. SIDDONS. By THOMAS CAMPBELL. 12mo. With a Portrait.

THE LIFE OF WICKLIF. By CHARLES WEBB LE BAS, A.M. 18mo. With a Portrait.

LUTHER AND THE LUTHERAN REFORMATION. By Rev. JOHN SCOTT, A.M. 2 vols. 18mo. Portraits.

THE LIFE OF ARCHBISHOP CRANMER. By CHARLES WEBB LE BAS, A.M. 2 vols. 18mo. With a Portrait.

THE RELIGIOUS OPINIONS AND CHARACTER OF WASHINGTON. By Rev. E. C. M'GUIRE. 12mo.

A LIFE OF GEORGE WASHINGTON. In Latin Prose. By FRANCIS GLASS, A.M., of Ohio. Edited by J. N. REYNOLDS. 12mo. Portrait.

THE LIFE OF ANDREW JACKSON, President of the United States of America. By WILLIAM COBBETT, M.P. 18mo. With a Portrait.

MATTHIAS AND HIS IMPOSTURES; or, the Progress of Fanaticism. Illustrated in the Extraordinary Case of Robert Matthews, and some of his Forerunners a Disciples. By WILLIAM L. STON 18mo.

LIVES OF THE NECROMA CERS; or, an Account of the mc Eminent Persons in Successive Ag who have claimed for themselves, to whom has been imputed by othei the Exercise of Magical Power. WILLIAM GODWIN. 12mo.

SKETCHES AND ECCENTR CITIES OF COL. DAVID CROC ETT. 12mo.

ANECDOTES OF SIR WA TER SCOTT. By the Ettri Shepherd. With a Life of the A thor, by S. DEWITT BLOODGOO Esq. 12mo.

THE LIFE OF BARON CUV ER. By Mrs. LEE. 12mo.

THE LIFE, CHARACTER, A LITERARY LABOURS OF SA UEL DREW, A.M. By his elde Son. 12mo.

MY IMPRISONMENTS: M MOIRS OF SILVIO PELLIC DA SALUZZO. Translated fr the Italian. By THOMAS ROSCO 12mo.

THE LIFE OF NAPOLEO BONAPARTE. By J. G. LOC HART, Esq. 2 vols. 18mo. W Portraits.

THE LIFE OF NELSON. 1 ROBERT SOUTHEY, LL.D. 18m With a Portrait.

THE LIFE AND ACTIONS ALEXANDER THE GREAT. the Rev. J. WILLIAMS. 18mo. W a Map.

THE LIFE OF LORD BYRO By JOHN GALT. 18mo.

THE LIFE OF MOHAMME Founder of the Religion of Isla and of the Empire of the Saracer By the Rev. GEORGE BUSH, of Ne York. 18mo. Engravings.

THE LIFE AND TIMES GEORGE THE FOURTH. Wi Anecdotes of Distinguished Perso of the last Fifty Years. By Re GEORGE CROLY. 18mo.

LIVES OF THE MOST EM NENT PAINTERS AND SCUL TORS. By ALLAN CUNNINGHA Esq. 5 vols. 18mo. With Portrait

THE LIFE OF MARY, QUEEN OF SCOTS. By HENRY GLASSFORD BELL, Esq. 2 vols. 18mo. With a Portrait.

MEMOIRS OF THE EMPRESS JOSEPHINE. By JOHN S. MEMES, LL.D. 18mo. With Portraits.

LIFE OF SIR ISAAC NEWTON. By Sir DAVID BREWSTER, K.B., LL.D., F.R.S. 18mo. With Engravings.

THE COURT AND CAMP OF BONAPARTE. 18mo. With a Portrait.

LIVES AND VOYAGES OF DRAKE, CAVENDISH, AND DAMPIER. Including an Introductory View of the Earlier Discoveries in the South Seas, and the History of the Bucaniers. 18mo. With Portraits.

MEMOIRS OF CELEBRATED FEMALE SOVEREIGNS. By Mrs. JAMESON. 2 vols. 18mo.

LIVES OF CELEBRATED TRAVELLERS. By JAMES AUGUSTUS ST. JOHN. 3 vols. 18mo.

LIFE OF FREDERICK THE SECOND, King of Prussia. By Lord DOVER. 2 vols. 18mo. With a Portrait.

INDIAN BIOGRAPHY; or, an Historical Account of those Individuals who have been distinguished among the North American Natives as Orators, Warriors, Statesmen, and other Remarkable Characters. By B. B. THATCHER, Esq. 2 vols. 18mo. With a Portrait.

HISTORY OF CHARLEMAGNE. To which is prefixed an Introduction, comprising the History of France from the earliest Period to the Birth of Charlemagne. By G. P. R. JAMES. 18mo. Portrait.

THE LIFE OF OLIVER CROMWELL. By the Rev. M. RUSSELL, LL.D. 2 vols. 18mo. Portrait.

MEMOIR OF THE LIFE OF PETER THE GREAT. By JOHN BARROW, Esq. 18mo. Portrait.

A LIFE OF WASHINGTON. By J. K. PAULDING, Esq. 2 vols. 18mo. With Engravings.

THE LIFE AND WORKS OF DR. FRANKLIN. 2 vols. 18mo. With a Portrait.

THE PURSUIT OF KNOWEDGE UNDER DIFFICULTIE its Pleasures and Rewards. Illu trated by Memoirs of Eminent Me 2 vols. 18mo.

THE LIFE AND TRAVELS MUNGO PARK; to which is ad ed an Account of his Death from t Journal of Isaaco, and the Substan of later Discoveries relative to t lamented Fate. 18mo. Engravin

AMERICAN BIOGRAPH Edited by JARED SPARKS, Esq. vols. 12mo. With a Portrait in ea volume.

I. Life of John Stark, by Edwa Everett.—Life of Charles Brockd Brown, by William H. Prescott. Life of Richard Montgomery, by Armstrong.—Life of Ethan Allen, Jared Sparks.

II. Life of Alexander Wilson, Wm. B. O. Peabody.—Life of Ca tain John Smith, by George S. H hard.

III. Life and Treason of Benedi Arnold, by Jared Sparks.

IV. Life of Anthony Wayne, John Armstrong —Life of Sir Hen Vane, by C. W. Upham.

V. Life of John Eliot, the Apos to the Indians, by Convers Franci

VI. Life of William Pinkney, Henry Wheaton.—Life of Willia Ellery, by E. T. Channing.—Life Cotton Mather, by Wm. B. O. Pe body.

VII. Life of Sir William Phips, Francis Bowen.—Life of Israel P nam, by W. B. O. Peabody.—M moir of Lucretia Maria Davidson, Miss Sedgwick.—Life of David R tenhouse, by James Renwick.

VIII. Life of Jonathan Edwar by Samuel Miller.—Life of Dav Brainerd, by Wm. B. O. Peabody.

IX. Life of Baron Steuben, Francis Bowen.—Life of Sebasti Cabot, by Charles Hayward, Jr. Life of William Eaton, by Corneli C. Felton.

X. Life of Robert Fulton, by Pr fessor Renwick —Life of Hen Hudson, by Henry R. Cleveland. Life of Joseph Warren, by Alexa der H. Everett.—Life of Father M quette, by Jared Sparks.

LIVES of the SIGNERS of the DECLARATION of INDEPENDENCE. By N. Dwight. 12mo.

BIOGRAPHIES of DISTINGUISHED FEMALES. 2 vols. 18mo.

EXEMPLARY and INSTRUCTIVE BIOGRAPHY. 3 vols. 18mo.

LIFE and CORRESPONDENCE of DEWITT CLINTON. By Professor Renwick. 18mo. Portrait.

LIFE and CORRESPONDENCE of GENERAL ALEXAN-

DER HAMILTON. By Profes. Renwick. 18mo.

LIFE and CORRESPONDENCE of GOVERNOR JO JAY. By Professor Renwi 18mo.

LIVES of the APOSTL and EARLY MARTYRS of t CHURCH. 18mo. Engraving.

SKETCHES of the LIVES DISTINGUISHED FEMALE Written for Young Ladies, with View to their Mental and Moral I provement. By an American La 18mo. Portrait.

VOYAGES, TRAVELS, &c.

LETTERS from the OLD WORLD. By a Lady of New-York. 2 vols. 12mo.

TRAVELS in the UNITED STATES during the Years 1834, 5, 6, including a Summer Residence with the Pawnee Indians and a Visit to Cuba and the Azores. By the Hon. Charles Augustus Murray. 2 vols. 12mo.

EMBASSY to the EASTERN COURTS of SIAM, COCHINCHINA, and MUSCAT. By Edmund Roberts. 8vo.

VOYAGE of the UNITED STATES FRIGATE POTOMAC, under the command of Com. John Downes, during the Circumnavigation of the Globe, in the years 1831, 1832, 1833, and 1834; including a particular Account of the Engagement at Quallah-Battoo, on the coast of Sumatra; with all the official Documents relating to the same. By J. N. Reynolds. 8vo. With Engravings

TRAVELS in EUROPE: viz., in England, Ireland, Scotland, France, Italy, Switzerland, some parts of Germany, and the Netherlands, during the Years 1835 and '36. By Wilbur Fisk, D.D. 8vo. Engravings.

RETROSPECT of WESTERN TRAVEL. By Miss Harriet Martineau. 2 vols. 12mo.

The FAR WEST; or, a To beyond the Mountains. 2 vo 12mo.

INCIDENTS of TRAVEL EGYPT, ARABIA PETRÆ and the HOLY LAND. By American. 2 vols. 12mo. Engi vings.

INCIDENTS of TRAVEL GREECE, TURKEY, RUSSI and POLAND. By the Author "Incidents of Travel in Egypt, A bia Petræa, and the Holy Land." vols. 12mo. Engravings.

A YEAR in SPAIN. By Young American. 3 vols. 12m Engravings. .

SPAIN REVISITED. By t Author of "A Year in Spain." vols. 12mo. Engravings.

The AMERICAN in EN LAND. By the Author of "A Ye in Spain." 2 vols. 12mo.

TRAVELS and RESEARC ES in CAFFRARIA; describi the Character, Customs, and Mo Condition of the Tribes inhabiti that Portion of Southern Afric By Stephen Kay. 12mo. Ma &c.

POLYNESIAN RESEARC ES, during a Residence of near eight Years in the Society and San wich Islands. By William Elli 4 vols. 12mo. Maps, &c.

GREAT BRITAIN, FRANCE, AND BELGIUM. A short Tour in 1835. By HEMAN HUMPHREY, D.D. 2 vols. 12mo.

A NARRATIVE OF FOUR VOYAGES to the South Sea, North and South Pacific Ocean, Chinese Sea, Ethiopic and Southern Atlantic Ocean, and Antarctic Ocean From the Year 1822 to 1831. Comprising an Account of some valuable Discoveries, including the Massacre Islands, where thirteen of the Author's Crew were massacred and eaten by Cannibals. By Capt. BENJAMIN MORRELL, Jun. 8vo.

NARRATIVE OF A VOYAGE TO THE SOUTH SEAS, in 1829-31. By ABBY JANE MORRELL, who accompanied her husband, Capt. Benjamin Morrell, Jun., of the Schooner Antarctic. 12mo.

PARIS AND THE PARISIANS, in 1835. By FRANCES TROLLOPE. 8vo. Engravings.

THE NARRATIVE OF ARTHUR GORDON PYM of Nantucket. Comprising the Details of a Mutiny and atrocious Butchery on board the American Brig Grampus, on her way to the South Seas, in the Month of June, 1827. With an Account of the Recapture of the Vessel by the Survivers; their Shipwreck and subsequent horrible Sufferings from Famine; their Deliverance by means of the British Schooner Jane Guy; the brief cruise of this latter Vessel in the Antarctic Ocean; her Capture, and the Massacre of her Crew, among a Group of Islands in the *eighty-fourth Parallel of Southern Latitude;* together with the incredible Adventures and Discoveries *still farther South* to which that distressing Calamity gave rise. 12mo.

NARRATIVE OF AN EXPEDITION THROUGH THE UPPER MISSISSIPPI TO ITASCA LAKE, the actual Source of this River; embracing an Exploratory Trip through the St Croix and Burntwood (or Broulé) Rivers. By HENRY R. SCHOOLCRAFT. 8vo. Maps.

A HOME TOUR THROUGH THE MANUFACTURING DISTRICTS OF ENGLAND. By Sir GEORGE HEAD. 12mo.

SKETCHES OF TURKEY i 1831 and 1832. By an American 8vo. Engravings.

LETTERS FROM THE ÆGEA By JAMES EMERSON, Esq. 8vo.

FOUR YEARS IN GREA BRITAIN. By CALVIN COLTO 12mo.

THE SOUTHWEST. By Yankee. 2 vols. 12mo.

THE RAMBLER IN NORT AMERICA. By C. J. LATROB Author of the "Alpenstock," &c. vols. 12mo.

THE RAMBLER IN MEXIC By C. J. LATROBE. 12mo.

A NARRATIVE OF THE VISI TO THE AMERICAN CHURC ES, by the Deputation from the Co gregational Union of England an Wales. By ANDREW REED, D.D and JAMES MATHESON, D.D. 2 vol 12mo.

CONSTANTINOPLE AND I1 ENVIRONS. In a Series of Le ters, exhibiting the actual State the Manners, Customs, and Habi of the Turks, Armenians, Jews, an Greeks, as modified by the policy Sultan Mahmoud. By an America long resident at Constantinop (Commodore PORTER). In 2 vol 12mo.

THE TOURIST, or Pocket Ma ual for Travellers on the Hudso River, the Western Canal and Stag Road to Niagara Falls, down Lak Ontario and the St. Lawrence Montreal and Quebec. Comprisin also the Routes to Lebanon, Bal ston, and Saratoga Springs. 18m With a Map.

NARRATIVE OF VOYAGES 1 EXPLORE THE SHORES o AFRICA, ARABIA, AND MAD GASCAR; performed in H. N Ships Leven and Barracouta, und the Direction of Captain W. F. OWEN, R N. 2 vols. 12mo.

A WINTER IN THE WES By a New-Yorker (C. F. HOFFMA Esq.). 2 vols. 12mo.

OBSERVATIONS ON PR FESSIONS, LITERATUR MANNERS, AND EMIGRATIO in the United States and Canad By the Rev. ISAAC FIDLER. 12m

9

AN IMPROVED MAP of the HUDSON RIVER, with the Post Roads between New-York and Albany.

THINGS as THEY ARE; or, Notes of a Traveller through some of the Middle and Northern States. 12mo. Engravings.

VISITS and SKETCHES at HOME and ABROAD. With Tales and Miscellanies now first collected, and a new Edition of the "Diary of an Ennuyée." By Mrs. JAMESON. 2 vols. 12mo.

A SUBALTERN'S FURLOUGH: Descriptive of Scenery in various parts of the United States, Upper and Lower Canada, New-Brunswick, and Nova Scotia, during the Summer and Autumn of 1832. By E. T. COKE, Lieutenant of the 45th Regiment. 2 vols. 12mo.

NARRATIVE of DISCOVERY and ADVENTURE in the POLAR SEAS and REGIONS. With Illustrations of their Climate, Geology, and Natural History, and an Account of the Whale-Fishery. By Professors LESLIE and JAMESON, and HUGH MURRAY. 18mo. With Maps, &c.

NARRATIVE of DISCOVERY and ADVENTURE in AFRICA. From the earliest Ages to the present Time. With Illustrations of its Geology, Mineralogy, and Zoology. By Professor JAMESON, and JAMES WILSON and HUGH MURRAY, Esqrs. 18mo.

DESCRIPTION of PI CAIRN'S ISLAND, and its Inha itants. With an Authentic Accou of the Mutiny of the Ship Bount and of the subsequent Fortunes the Mutineers. By J. BARRO Esq. 18mo. Engravings.

JOURNAL of an EXPED TION to EXPLORE th COURSE and TERMINATIO OF THE NIGER. With a Narr tive of a Voyage down that River its Termination. By RICHARD a JOHN LANDER. 2 vols. 18mo. E gravings.

THE TRAVELS and R SEARCHES of ALEXANDE VON HUMBOLDT; being a co densed Narrative of his Journeys the Equinoctial Regions of Americ and in Asiatic Russia: together wi Analyses of his more important I vestigations. By W. MACGILL VRAY, A.M. 18mo. Engravings.

PARRY'S VOYAGES an JOURNEY towards th NORTH POLE. 2 vols. 18m Engravings.

PERILS of the SEA; bein Authentic Narratives of Remark ble and Affecting Disasters upon th Deep. With Illustrations of th Power and Goodness of God in wo derful Preservations. 18mo. E gravings.

CAROLINE WESTERLEY or, the Young Traveller from Ohi By Mrs. PHELPS (formerly Mrs. LI COLN). 18mo. Engravings.

THEOLOGY, &c.

THE WORKS of the REV. ROBERT HALL, A.M. With a brief Memoir of his Life, by Dr. GREGORY, and Observations on his Character as a Preacher, by the Rev. JOHN FOSTER. Edited by OLINTHUS GREGORY, LL.D. 3 vols. 8vo. Portrait.

ESSAYS on the PRINCIPLES of MORALITY, and on the Private and Political Rights and Obligations of Mankind. By JONATHAN DYMOND. With a Preface by the Rev. GEORGE BUSH, M.A. 8vo.

EVIDENCE of the TRUT of the CHRISTIAN RELIGION derived from the literal Fulfilment o Prophecy. By the Rev. ALEXANDE KEITH. 12mo.

DEMONSTRATION of th TRUTH of the CHRISTIA RELIGION. By ALEX. KEITH D.D. 12mo. Engravings.

THE HARMONY of CHRIS TIAN FAITH and CHRISTIA CHARACTER, and the Culture an Discipline of the Mind. By JOH ABERCROMBIE, M.D. 18mo.

INSTITUTES of ECCLESIASTICAL HISTORY, Ancient and Modern, in four Books, much Corrected, Enlarged, and Improved, from the Primary Authorities, by JOHN LAWRENCE VON MOSHEIM, D.D., Chancellor of the University of Gottingen. A new and literal Translation from the original Latin, with copious additional Notes, original and selected. By JAMES MURDOCK, D.D. 3 vols. 8vo.

A HISTORY of the CHURCH, from the earliest Ages to the Reformation. By the Rev. GEORGE WADDINGTON, M.A. 8vo.

PRIDEAUX'S CONNEXIONS; or, the Old and New Testaments connected, in the History of the Jews and neighbouring Nations, from the Declension of the Kingdoms of Israel and Judah to the Time of Christ. By HUMPHREY PRIDEAUX, D.D. New Edition. 2 vols. 8vo. With Maps and Engravings.

HISTORY of PRIESTCRAFT in all Ages and Countries. By WILLIAM HOWITT. 12mo.

A NARRATIVE of EVENT CONNECTED WITH THE RISE AN PROGRESS of the PROTES TANT EPISCOPAL CHURC IN VIRGINIA. To which is adde an Appendix, containing the Jou nals of the Conventions in Virgini from the Commencement to the pres ent Time. By F. L. HAWKS. 8vo.

LUTHER AND THE LUTHER AN REFORMATION. By th Rev. JOHN SCOTT, A.M. 2 vol 18mo. Portraits.

HISTORY of THE REFORM ED RELIGION IN FRANCE By the Rev. E. SMEDLEY. 3 vol 18mo. Engravings.

HISTORY of THE BIBLE. B the Rev. G. R. GLEIG. 2 vol 18mo. Map.

SACRED HISTORY of TH WORLD, as displayed in the Crea tion and Subsequent Events to th Deluge. Attempted to be Philc sophically considered in a Series c Letters to a Son. By SHARO TURNER, F.S.A. 3 vols. 18mo.

NATURAL THEOLOGY.

PALEY'S NATURAL THEOLOGY. With Illustrative Notes, by HENRY LORD BROUGHAM, F.R.S., and Sir CHARLES BELL, K.G.H., F.R.S., L. & E. With numerous Woodcuts. To which are added Preliminary Observations and Notes. By ALONZO POTTER, D.D. 2 vols. 18mo.

ON THE POWER, WISDOM, AND GOODNESS of GOD, as manifested in the Adaptation of External Nature to the Moral and In-

tellectual Constitution of Man. B the Rev. THOMAS CHALMERS, D.D Professor of Divinity in the Univer sity of Edinburgh. 12mo.

THE HAND, its Mechanism an Vital Endowments, as evincing De sign. By Sir CHARLES BELI K.G.H., F.R.S., &c. 12mo.

ON ASTRONOMY AND GEN ERAL PHYSICS. By the Re WILLIAM WHEWELL. M.A., F.R.S &c. 12mo.

PROTESTANT JESUITISM. By a Protestant. 12mo.

THOUGHTS ON THE RELIGIOUS STATE of THE COUNTRY: with Reasons for preferring Episcopacy. By the Rev. CALVIN COLTON. 12mo.

A CONCORDANCE TO THE HOLY SCRIPTURES of the Old and New Testaments. By JOHN BROWN, of Haddington. 32mo.

THE CONSISTENCY of TH WHOLE SCHEME of REVE LATION with Itself and with Hu man Reason. By PHILIP NICH LAS SHUTTLEWORTH, D.D. 18mo

HELP TO FAITH; or, a Sum mary of the Evidences of the Ger uineness, Authenticity, Credibility and Divine Authority of the Hol Scriptures. By the Rev. P. F SANDFORD. 12mo.

A DICTIONARY OF THE HOLY BIBLE. Containing an Historical Account of the Persons; a Geographical and Historical Account of the Places; a Literal, Critical, and Systematical Description of other Objects, whether Natural, Artificial, Civil, Religious, or Military; and an Explanation of the appellative Terms mentioned in the Old and New Testaments By the Rev JOHN BROWN. With a Life of the Author; and an Essay on the Evidence of Christianity. 8vo.

SERMONS OF THE REV. JAMES SAURIN, late Pastor of the French Church at the Hague. From the French, by the Rev. ROBERT ROBINSON, Rev. HENRY HUNTER, D.D., and Rev. JOSEPH SUTCLIFFE, A.M. A new Edition, with additional Sermons. Revised and corrected by the Rev. SAMUEL BURDER, A.M. With a likeness of the Author, and a general Index. From the last London Edition. With a Preface by the Rev. J. P. K. HENSHAW, D.D. 2 vols. 8vo.

WORKS OF THE REV. JOHN WESLEY. 10 vols. 8vo.

A TREATISE ON THE MILLENIUM; in which the prevailing Theories on that Subject are carefully examined; and the true Scriptural Doctrine attempted to be elicited and established. By GEORGE BUSH, A.M. 12mo.

THE COMFORTER; or, Extracts selected for the Consolation of Mourners under the Bereavement of Friends and Relations. By a Village Pastor. 12mo.

CHRISTIANITY INDEPENDENT OF THE CIVIL GOVERNMENT. 12mo.

SUNDAY EVENINGS; or, an easy Introduction to the Reading of the Bible. By the Author of "The Infant Christian's First Catechism." 18mo. Engravings.

EVIDENCES OF CHRISTIANITY; or, Uncle Philip's Conversations with the Children about the Truth of the Christian Religion. 18mo. Engravings.

MEDICINE, SURGERY, &c.

THE STUDY OF MEDICINE. By JOHN MASON GOOD, M.D., F.R.S. Improved from the Author's Manuscripts, and by Reference to the latest Advances in Physiology, Pathology, and Practice. By SAMUEL COOPER, M.D. With Notes, by A. SIDNEY DOANE, A.M., M.D. To which is prefixed, a Sketch of the History of Medicine, from its Origin to the Commencement of the 19th Century. By J. BOSTOCK, M.D., F.R.S. 2 vols. 8vo.

MIDWIFERY ILLUSTRATED. By J. P. MAYGRIER, M.D. Translated from the French, with Notes, by A. SIDNEY DOANE, A.M., M.D. With 82 Plates. 8vo.

SURGERY ILLUSTRATED. Compiled from the Works of Cutler, Hind, Velpeau, and Blasius. By A. SIDNEY DOANE, A.M., M.D. With 52 Plates. 8vo.

A TREATISE ON TOPOGRAPHICAL ANATOMY; or, the Anatomy of the Regions of the Human Body, considered in its Relations with Surgery and Operative Medicine. With an Atlas of 1' Plates. By PH. FRED. BLANDIN, Professor of Anatomy and Operative Medicine, &c. Translated from the French, by A. SIDNEY DOANE, A.M. M.D. With additional Matter and Plates. 8vo.

ELEMENTS OF THE ETIOLOGY AND PHILOSOPHY O EPIDEMICS. By JOSEPH MATHER SMITH, M.D. 8vo.

AN ELEMENTARY TREATISE ON ANATOMY. By A. L. J. BAYLE. Translated from the sixth French Edition, by A. SIDNEY DOANE, A.M., M.D. 18mo.

LEXICON MEDICUM; or Medical Dictionary. By R. HOOPER, M.D. With Additions from American Authors, by SAMUEL AKERLY, M.D. 8vo.

A DICTIONARY OF PRACTICAL SURGERY. By S. Cooper, M.D. With numerous Notes and Additions, embracing all the principal American Improvements. By D. M. Reese, M.D. 8vo.

A TREATISE on EPIDEMI CHOLERA, as observed in t Duane-street Cholera Hospit New-York, during its Prevalen there in 1834. By F. T. Ferr 8vo. Plates.

DIRECTIONS for INVIGO-RATING AND PROLONGING LIFE; or, the Invalid's Oracle. By William Kitchiner, M.D. Improved by T. S. Barrett, M.D. 18mo.

THE ECONOMY OF HEALTH or, the Stream of Human Life, from the Cradle to the Grave. With Reflections, Moral, Physical, and Philosophical, on the Septennial Phases of Human Existence. By James Johnson. 18mo.

THE PRINCIPLES OF PHYSIOLOGY applied to the Preservation of Health, and to the Improveme of Physical and Mental Educati By Andrew Combe, M.D. 18 Engravings.

THE PHILOSOPHY OF LI ING; or, the Way to enjoy Life a its Comforts. By Caleb Tickno A.M., M.D. 18mo. Engravings.

ANIMAL MECHANISM A PHYSIOLOGY; being a Plain a Familiar Exposition of the Structu and Functions of the Human Syste Designed for the Use of Families a Schools. By John H. Grisco M.D. 18mo. Engravings.

FOR SCHOOLS AND COLLEGES.

ANTHON'S SERIES OF CLASSICAL WORKS.

FIRST LATIN LESSONS, containing the most important Parts of the Grammar of the Latin Language, together with appropriate Exercises in the translating and writing of Latin, for the Use of Beginners. By Charles Anthon, LL.D., &c. 12mo.

FIRST GREEK LESSONS, containing the most important Parts of the Grammar of the Greek Language, together with appropriate Exercises in the translating and writing of Greek, for the Use of Beginners. By Charles Anthon, LL.D. 12mo.

A GRAMMAR OF THE GREEK LANGUAGE, for the Use of Schools and Colleges. By Charles Anthon, LL.D. 12mo.

THE GREEK READER. By Frederic Jacobs. A New Edition, with English Notes, critical and explanatory, a Metrical Index to Homer and Anacreon, and a copious Lexicon. By Charles Anthon, LL.D., &c. 12mo.

A SYSTEM OF GREEK PRO ODY AND METRE, for the U of Schools and Colleges; togeth with the Choral Scanning of t Prometheus Vinctus of Æschylu and the Ajax and Œdipus Tyrann of Sophocles; to which are apper ed Remarks on the Indo-Germa Analogies. By Charles Antho LL.D. 12mo.

CÆSAR'S COMMENTARI on the GALLIC WAR; and t first Book of the Greek Paraphras with English Notes, critical and planatory, Plans of Battles, Sieg &c., and Historical, Geographic and Archæological Indexes. Charles Anthon, LL.D. 12 Map, Portrait, &c.

SALLUST'S JUGURTHI WAR AND CONSPIRACY CATILINE. With an Eng Commentary, and Geographical Historical Indexes. By Charl Anthon, LL.D. Ninth Edition, c rected and enlarged. 12mo. P trait.

13

SELECT ORATIONS OF CI-CERO. With English Notes, critical and explanatory, and Historical, Geographical, and Legal Indexes. By CHARLES ANTHON, LL.D., &c. A new Edition, with Improvements. 12mo. With a Portrait.

THE WORKS OF HORACE. With English Notes, critical and explanatory. By CHARLES AN-THON, LL.D., &c. New Edition, with corrections and improvements. 12mo.

A CLASSICAL DICTIONAR containing an Account of all th Proper Names mentioned in Ancie Authors, and intended to elucida all the Important Points connecte with the Geography, History, Bio raphy, Archæology, and Mytholog of the Greeks and Romans, togeth with a copious Chronological Tabl and an Account of the Coin Weights, and Measures of the A cients, with Tabular Values of th same. By CHARLES ANTHOI LL.D., &c. 8vo. (Nearly ready

A LIFE OF GEORGE WASH-INGTON. In Latin Prose. By FRANCIS GLASS, A.M., of Ohio. Edited by J. N. REYNOLDS. 12mo. Portrait.

INITIA LATINA; or, the Rudiments of the Latin Tongue. Illustrated by Progressive Exercises. By CHARLES H. LYON. 12mo.

OUTLINES OF IMPERFECT AND DISORDERED MENTAL ACTION. By THOMAS C. UPHAM, Professor of Mental and Moral Philosophy in Bowdoin College. 18mo.

MENTAL PHILOSOPHY; embracing the three Departments of the Intellect, Sensibilities, and Will. By THOMAS C. UPHAM. 3 vols. 12mo.

A PHILOSOPHICAL AND PRACTICAL TREATISE ON THE WILL. By Professor UPHAM.

INQUIRIES CONCERNING THE INTELLECTUAL POWERS, and the Investigation of Truth. By JOHN ABERCROMBIE, M.D., F.R.S. With Questions. 18mo.

THE PHILOSOPHY OF THE MORAL FEELINGS. By JOHN ABERCROMBIE, M.D., F.R.S. With Questions. 18mo.

PALEY'S NATURAL THE-OLOGY. With Illustrative Notes, by HENRY LORD BROUGHAM, F.R.S., and Sir CHARLES BELL, K.G.H., F.R.S., L. & E. With numerous Woodcuts. To which are added Preliminary Observations and Notes. By ALONZO POTTER, D.D. 2 vols. 18mo.

FAMILIAR ILLUSTRATIONS OF NATURAL PHILOSOPHY, selected principally from Daniell's

Chemical Philosophy. By JAMES RENWICK, LL.D. 18mo. Wit numerous Engravings.

FIRST PRINCIPLES O CHEMISTRY familiarly explaine By Professor RENWICK. 18m With numerous Illustrative Engr vings.

ILLUSTRATIONS OF ME CHANICS. By Professors MOSE LEY and RENWICK. 18mo. Engra vings.

THE SCIENCE OF MECHAN ICS applied to Practical Purpose By JAMES RENWICK, LL.D. 18m Engravings.

THE ELEMENTS OF GEOL OGY, for Popular Use; containin a Description of the Geological For mation and Mineral Resources of th United States. By CHARLES A LEE, A.M., M.D. 18mo. Engra vings.

THE PRINCIPLES OF PHYSI OLOGY applied to the Preservatio of Health, and to the Improvemen of Physical and Mental Education By ANDREW COMBE, M.D. 18mo Engravings.

ANIMAL MECHANISM AN PHYSIOLOGY; being a plain an familiar Exposition of the Structur and Functions of the Human System Designed for the Use of Families an Schools. By JOHN H. GRISCOM M.D. 18mo. Engravings.

UNIVERSAL HISTORY, fro the Creation of the World to the De cease of George III., 1820. By the Hon. ALEXANDER FRASER TYTLER and Rev. E. NARES, D D. Edited by an American. 6 vols. 18mo.

AMERICAN HISTORY. By the Author of " American Popular Lessons." 3 vols. 18mo. Engravings.

THE HISTORY OF GREECE. By Dr. GOLDSMITH. Edited by the Author of " American Popular Lessons," &c. 18mo.

THE HISTORY OF ROME. By Dr. GOLDSMITH. Edited by H. W. HERBERT, Esq. 18mo.

AN ELEMENTARY TREATISE ON MECHANICS. Trans-

lated from the French of M. B[c] CHARLAT. With Additions and E[endations, designed to adapt it to t[Use of the Cadets of the U. S. M[itary Academy. By EDWARD COURTENAY. 8vo.

COBB'S SCHOOL BOOK[Including Walker's Dictionary, [F planatory Arithmetic, Nos. I and North American Reader, &c.

A TABLE OF LOGARITHM[OF LOGARITHMIC SINES, [A] [A] TRAVERSE TABLE. 12m[

NATURAL PHILOSOPHY.

A PRELIMINARY DISCOURSE ON THE STUDY OF NATURAL PHILOSOPHY. By JOHN FREDERIC WILLIAM HERSCHEL, A.M., &c. 12mo.

FAMILIAR ILLUSTRATIONS OF NATURAL PHILOSOPHY, selected principally from Daniell's Chemical Philosophy. By JAMES RENWICK, LL D. 18mo. With numerous Engravings.

LETTERS ON NATURAL MAGIC. Addressed to Sir Walter Scott. By Sir DAVID BREWSTER. 18mo. With Engravings.

LETTERS OF EULER on Different Subjects of Natural Philosophy. Addressed to a German Princess. Translated by HUNTER. With Notes, and a Life of Euler, by Sir DAVID BREWSTER; with additional Notes, by JOHN GRISCOM, LL.D. With a Glossary of Scientific Terms. 2 vols. 18mo. Engravings.

ON ASTRONOMY AND GENERAL PHYSICS. By the Rev WILLIAM WHEWELL. M.A., F.R.S., &c. 12mo.

THE EARTH: its Physical Condition and most Remarkable Phenomena. By W. MULLINGER HIGGINS. 18mo. Engravings.

CELESTIAL SCENERY; or, the Wonders of the Planetary System displayed. Illustrating the Per-

fections of Deity and a Plurality [Worlds. By THOMAS DICK, LL. 18mo. Engravings.

THE SIDEREAL HEAVEN[and other Subjects connected wi[Astronomy, as illustrative of t[Character of the Deity, and of an [finity of Worlds. By THOMAS DIC[LL.D. 18mo. Engravings.

AN ELEMENTARY TRE[TISE ON MECHANICS. Tran[lated from the French of M. Bo[CHARLAT. With Additions and E[endations, designed to adapt it to [Use of the Cadets of the U. S. M[itary Academy. By EDWARD COURTENAY. 8vo.

ILLUSTRATIONS OF M[CHANICS. By Professors Mos[LEY and RENWICK. 18mo. Engr[vings.

THE SCIENCE OF MECHA[ICS applied to Practical Purpose[By JAMES RENWICK, LL.D. 18m[Engravings.

CHAPTAL'S CHYMISTRY [A] PLIED TO AGRICULTURE. New Translation, with valuable S[lections from Sir HUMPHREY DAV[and others.

FIRST PRINCIPLES [CHEMISTRY familiarly explaine[By Professor RENWICK. 18m[With numerous Illustrative Engr[vings.

15

NATURAL HISTORY.

A POPULAR GUIDE TO THE OBSERVATION OF NATURE; or, Hints of Inducement to the Study of Natural Productions and Appearances, in their Connexions and Relations. By ROBERT MUDIE. 18mo. Engravings.

NATURAL HISTORY; or, Uncle Philip's Conversations with the Children about Tools and Trades among the Inferior Animals. 18mo. With Illustrative Engravings.

THE HAND, its Mechanism and Vital Endowments, as evincing Design. By Sir CHARLES BELL, K.G.H., F.R.S.L. & E, &c. 12mo.

THE NATURAL HISTORY OF QUADRUPEDS. 18mo. Numerous Engravings.

THE ELEPHANT as he exists in a Wild State, and as he has been made subservient, in Peace and in War, to the Purposes of Man. 18mo. Illustrated by numerous Engravings.

THE NATURAL HISTORY OF BIRDS; their Architecture, Habits, &c. 18mo. With numerous Illustrative Engravings.

THE NATURAL HISTORY INSECTS. 2 vols. 18mo. Engravings.

A MANUAL OF CONCHOLGY, according to the System laid down by Lamarck, with the late improvements by De Blainville. Examplified and arranged for the U of Students. By THOMAS WYAT M.A. Illustrated by 36 Plates, containing more than two hundred Types drawn from the Natural Shell. 8vo.
Also an Edition with colour Plates.

THE AMERICAN FORES or, Uncle Philip's Conversatio with the Children about the Tre of America. 18mo. With numero Engravings.

VEGETABLE SUBSTANCE used for the Food of Man. 18m With numerous Engravings.

THE ELEMENTS OF GEO OGY, for Popular Use; containu a Description of the Geological Fo mation and Mineral Resources of t United States. By CHARLES LEE, A.M., M.D. 18mo. Engravings.

POETRY, AND THE DRAMA.

POEMS, by WILLIAM CULLEN BRYANT. New Edition, enlarged. 12mo. With a Vignette.

FANNY, with other Poems. By FITZ-GREENE HALLECK. 12mo. With a Vignette.

POEMS, by FITZ-GREENE HALLECK, Esq. 12mo. Vignette.

THE RIVALS OF ESTE, and other Poems. By JAMES G. BROOKS and MARY E. BROOKS. 12mo.

SELECTIONS FROM THE AMERICAN POETS. By W. C. BRYANT, Esq. 18mo.

SELECTIONS FROM FOREIGN POETS. By FITZ-GREENE HALLECK, Esq. 2 vols. 18mo.

THE SIAMESE TWINS. A Satirical Tale of the Times, &c. By Sir LYTTON BULWER. 12mo.

VIRGIL. The Eclogues translated by WRANGHAM, the Georgics SOTHEBY, and the Æneid by DRYDEN. 2 vols. 18mo. Portrait.

HORACE. Translated by PHIL. FRANCIS, D.D. With an Appendi containing Translations of variou Odes. &c., by BEN JONSON, COLEY, MILTON, DRYDEN, POPE, ADISON, SWIFT, BENTLEY, CHATTERTON, G. WAKEFIELD, PORSO BYRON, &c., and by some of th most eminent Poets of the preser Day. And

PHÆDRUS. With the Appendix of GUDIUS. Translated t CHRISTOPHER SMART, A.M. 2 vol 18mo. With a Portrait.

OVID. Translated by DRYDE POPE, CONGREVE, ADDISON, an others. 2 vols. 18mo. Portrait.

THE REBEL, and other Tales. By Sir LYTTON BULWER, M.P. 12mo.

ATALANTIS: A Story of the Sea. By W. GILMORE SIMMS, Esq. 8vo.

HOMER. Translated by ALEXANDER POPE, Esq. 3 vols. 18mo. Portrait

JUVENAL. Translated by CHARLES BADHAM, M.D., F.R.S. New Edition. With an Appendix, containing Imitations of the Third and Tenth Satires. By Dr. SAMUEL JOHNSON. And

PERSIUS. Translated by the Rt. Hon. Sir W. DRUMMOND, F.R.S. 18mo. Portrait.

PINDAR. Translated by the Rev. C. A. WHEELWRIGHT. And

ANACREON. Translated by THOMAS BOURNE, Esq. 18mo. Portrait.

THE DRAMATIC WORKS AND POEMS OF WILLIAM SHAKSPEARE. With Notes, original and selected, and Introductory Remarks to each Play, by SAMUEL WELLER SINGER, F S.A., and a Life of the Poet, by CHARLES SYMMONS, D.D. 8vo. With numerous Engravings.

THE DRAMATIC WORKS OF WILLIAM SHAKSPEARE, with the Corrections and Illustrations of Dr. JOHNSON, G. STEEVENS, and others. Revised by ISAAC REED, Esq. 6 vols. crown 8vo. With a Portrait and other Engravings.

VELASCO: a Tragedy, in fi Acts. By EPES SARGENT. 12m

THE PLAYS OF PHILIP MA SINGER. 3 vols. 18mo. With Portrait.

THE DRAMATIC WORKS JOHN FORD. With Notes, cr ical and explanatory. In 2 vo 18mo.

DRAMATIC SCENES FR REAL LIFE. By Lady MORGA 2 vols. 12mo.

THE DOOM OF DEVORGOI a Melo-Drama. AUCHINDRAN or, the Ayrshire Tragedy. By S WALTER SCOTT. 12mo.

ÆSCHYLUS. Translated the Rev. R. POTTER, M.A. 18mo

SOPHOCLES. Translated THOMAS FRANCKLIN, D.D. 18m With a Portrait.

EURIPIDES. Translated by t Rev. R. POTTER, M.A. 3 vols. 18m Portrait.

RICHELIEU; or, the Conspir cy: a Play, in five Acts. With H torical Odes. By Sir LYTTON BU WER. 12mo.

THE LADY OF LYONS: a Pla in five Acts. By Sir LYTTON BU WER. 12mo.

THE SEA-CAPTAIN; or, t Birthright. A Play, in five Act By Sir LYTTON BULWER. 12mo.

BLANCHE OF NAVARRE. Play, in five Acts. By G. P. JAMES, Esq. 12mo.

MISCELLANEOUS.

THE WORKS OF JOSEPH ADDISON. 3 vols. 8vo, embracing "The Spectator." Portrait.

THE WORKS OF HENRY MACKENZIE, Esq. Complete in one vol. 12mo. Portrait.

THE COMPLETE WORKS OF EDMUND BURKE. With a Memoir. 3 vols. 8vo. Portrait.

THE WORKS OF CHARLES LAMB. Complete—with his Life, by TALFOURD. In 2 vols. 12mo. Portrait.

THE WORKS OF JOHN DR DEN, in Verse and Prose. With Life, by the Rev. JOHN MITFOR 2 vols. 8vo. Portrait.

THE WORKS OF HANNA MORE. 7 vols. 12mo. Illustratio to each volume.

The same work in 2 vols. roy 8vo, with Illustrations.

Also an Edition in one vol. roy 8vo, with a Portrait, &c.

LITERARY REMAINS OF T LATE HENRY NEELE. 8vo.

THE WORKS OF LORD CHES-
TERFIELD, including his Letters
to his Son. With a Life of the Author. 8vo.

THE WRITINGS OF ROBERT
C. SANDS, in Prose and Verse.
With a Memoir of the Author. In 2
vols. 8vo. With a Portrait.

THE MISCELLANEOUS
WORKS OF REV. JOHN WES-
LEY. 3 vols. 8vo.

SELECTIONS FROM THE
WORKS OF DR. SAMUEL
JOHNSON. With a Life and Por-
trait. 2 vols. 18mo.

SELECTIONS FROM THE
WORKS OF DR. GOLDSMITH.
With a Life and Portrait. 18mo.

SELECTIONS FROM THE
WRITINGS OF WASHINGTON.
2 vols. 18mo.

SELECTIONS FROM THE
SPECTATOR: embracing the
most interesting Papers by ADDISON,
STEELE, and others. 2 vols. 18mo.

LETTERS, CONVERSA-
TIONS, AND RECOLLECTIONS
OF THE LATE S. T. COLERIDGE.
12mo.

SPECIMENS OF THE TABLE
TALK OF THE LATE SAMUEL
TAYLOR COLERIDGE. 12mo.

OUTLINES OF IMPERFECT
AND DISORDERED MENTAL
ACTION. By THOMAS C. UPHAM,
Professor of Mental and Moral Phi-
losophy in Bowdoin College. 18mo.

MENTAL PHILOSOPHY; em-
bracing the three Departments of the
Intellect, Sensibilities, and Will. By
THOMAS C. UPHAM. 3 vols. 12mo.

A PHILOSOPHICAL AND
PRACTICAL TREATISE ON
THE WILL. By Professor UPHAM.

INQUIRIES CONCERNING THE
INTELLECTUAL POWERS,
and the Investigation of Truth. By
JOHN ABERCROMBIE, M.D., F.R.S.
With Questions. 18mo.

THE PHILOSOPHY OF THE
MORAL FEELINGS. By JOHN
ABERCROMBIE, M.D., F.R.S. With
Questions. 18mo.

MINIATURE LEXICON OF
THE ENGLISH LANGUAGE.
By LYMAN COBB. 48mo.

ENGLISH SYNONYME
With copious Illustrations and E
planations, drawn from the b
Writers. By GEORGE CRABB, M
8vo.

INFANTRY TACTICS;
Rules for the Exercise and Mano
vres of the United States' Infant
New Edition. By Major-Gene
SCOTT, U. S. Army. [Published
Authority.] 3 vols. 18mo. Plate

THE PERCY ANECDOTE
Revised Edition. To which is ad
ed, a valuable Collection of Ame
can Anecdotes, original and selecte
8vo. Portraits.

ANECDOTES, Literary, Mor
Religious, and Miscellaneous. Co
piled by the Rev. Messrs. HOES a
WAY. 8vo.

ALGIC RESEARCHES. Co
prising Inquiries respecting the Me
tal Characteristics of the Nor
American Indians. First Seri
Indian Tales and Legends.
HENRY ROWE SCHOOLCRAFT.
vols. 12mo.

INDIAN TRAITS; bei
Sketches of the Manners, Custom
and Character of the North Ame
can Natives. By B. B. THATCHE
Esq. 2 vols. 18mo. Engravings.

GEORGIA SCENES. Ne
Edition. With original Illustr
tions. 12mo.

HOW TO OBSERVE. — MO
ALS AND MANNERS. By HA
RIET MARTINEAU. 12mo.

THE LETTERS OF THE BRI
ISH SPY. By WILLIAM WIR
Esq. To which is prefixed, a Bi
graphical Sketch of the Autho
12mo. Portrait.

ZION'S SONGSTER. Co
piled by the Rev. THOMAS MASO
48mo.

THE COOK'S ORACLE an
Housekeeper's Manual. Containir
Receipts for Cookery, and Directio
for Carving. With a Complete Sy
tem of Cookery for Catholic Fam
lies. By WILLIAM KITCHINE
M.D. 12mo.

MODERN AMERICAN COO
ERY. With a List of Family Me
ical Receipts, and a valuable M
cellany. By Miss P. SMITH. 16m

THE FAIRY BOOK. 16mo. Illustrated with 81 Woodcuts, by ADAMS.

A NEW HIEROGLYPHICAL BIBLE, with 400 Cuts, by ADAMS. 16mo.

THE LIFE AND SURPRISING ADVENTURES OF ROBINSON CRUSOE, of York, Mariner. With a Biographical Account of DE FOE. Illustrated with 50 characteristic Engravings, by ADAMS. 12mo.

THE PILGRIM'S PROGRESS. With a Life of BUNYAN, by ROBERT SOUTHEY, LL.D. New and beautiful Edition, splendidly illustrated with 50 Engravings, by ADAMS. 12mo.

THE LIFE OF CHRIST, in the Words of the Evangelists. A complete Harmony of the Gospel History of our Saviour. Small 4to. With 30 Engravings on Wood, by ADAMS.

EVENINGS AT HOME; or, the Juvenile Budget opened. By Dr AIKIN and Mrs. BARBAULD. Small 4to. With 34 Engravings on Wood.

THE FARMER'S INSTRUCT-ER; consisting of Essays, Practical Directions, and Hints for the Management of the Farm, Garden. &c. By the Hon. Judge BUEL. 2 vols. 18mo. With Engravings.

A TREATISE ON AGRICULTURE; comprising a Concise History of its Origin and Progress; the present Condition of the Art abroad and at home, and the Theory and Practice of Husbandry. To which is added a Dissertation on the Kitchen and Fruit Garden. By General JOHN ARMSTRONG. With Notes, by the Hon. Judge BUEL. 18mo.

THE USEFUL ARTS, popularly treated. 18mo. With numerous illustrative Woodcuts.

ENGLAND AND AMERICA. A Comparison of the Social and Political State of both Nations. 8vo.

FRANCE: SOCIAL, LITERARY, AND POLITICAL. By H. L. BULWER, Esq., M.P. 2 vols. 12mo.

ENGLAND AND THE ENGLISH. By Sir LYTTON BULWER, M.P. 2 vols. 12mo.

PUBLIC AND PRIVAT ECONOMY: Illustrated by Obs vations made in Europe in 183 In three Parts. By THEODO SEDGWICK. 3 vols. 12mo.

POLITICAL ECONOMY. Objects stated and explained, and Principles familiarly and practica illustrated. 18mo.

LETTERS TO YOUNG L DIES. By Mrs. L. H. SIGOURN 12mo.

LETTERS TO MOTHERS. Mrs. L. H. SIGOURNEY. 12mo.

DOMESTIC DUTIES; or, structions to Young Married Lad on the Management of their Hou holds, and the Regulation of th Conduct in the various Relations a Duties of Married Life. By M W. PARKES. With Improvemen 12mo.

SLAVERY IN THE UNIT STATES. By J. K. PAULDIN Esq. 18mo.

DISCOURSES AND ADDRES ES on Subjects of American Histo Arts, and Literature. By GULL C. VERPLANCK. 12mo.

LETTERS ON DEMONOLOG AND WITCHCRAFT. By WALTER SCOTT. 18mo. Eng ving.

FESTIVALS, GAMES, A AMUSEMENTS, Ancient and M ern. By HORATIO SMITH, E With Additions by SAMUEL WO WORTH, Esq., of New-York. 18n

LECTURES ON GENER LITERATURE, POETRY, & By JAMES MONTGOMERY. 18mo.

A TREATISE ON LA GUAGE; or, the Relations whi Words bear to Things. By A. JOHNSON. 12mo.

THE ORATIONS OF DEMO THENES. Translated by THOM LELAND, D.D. 2 vols. 18mo. P trait.

CICERO. The Orations tran lated by DUNCAN, the Offices COCKMAN, and the Cato and Læli by MELMOTH. 3 vols. 18mo. P trait.

THE PLEASURES AND A VANTAGES OF SCIENCE. ALONZO POTTER, D.D. 18mo.

ON THE IMPROVEMENT OF SOCIETY by the Diffusion of Knowledge. By THOMAS DICK, LL.D. 18mo.

PRACTICAL EDUCATION By RICHARD LOVELL EDGEWORTH and MARIA EDGEWORTH. 12mo.

THE DISTRICT SCHOOL. By J. O. TAYLOR. 12mo.

UNCLE PHILIP'S CONVER-SATIONS WITH THE CHILDREN ABOUT THE WHALE-FISHERY AND POLAR SEAS. 2 vols. 18mo. Numerous Engravings.

THE HOUSEHOLD BOOK. By the Rev. Dr. POTTER. 18mo.

EVENING READINGS IN NATURE AND MAN. Selected and arranged by ALONZO POTTER, D.D. 18mo.

A FAMILIAR TREATISE ON THE CONSTITUTION OF THE UNITED STATES. 18mo.

SKETCHES OF AMERICAN ENTERPRISE. 2 vols. 18mo.

THE WONDERS OF NATURE AND ART. 18mo. Numerous Engravings.

THE POOR RICH MAN AND THE RICH POOR MAN. By Miss C. M. SEDGWICK. 18mo.

THE SWISS FAMILY ROB-INSON; or, Adventures of a Father and Mother and Four Sons on a Desert Island. The Progress of the Story forming a clear Illustration of the First Principles of Natural His-tory, and many Branches of Science which most immediately apply to the Business of Life. 2 vols. 18mo. Engravings.

LIVE AND LET LIVE. By Miss C. M. SEDGWICK. 18mo.

THE SON OF A GENIUS. Tale for the Use of Youth. By M Hopland. 18mo. Engravings.

THE YOUNG CRUSOE; the Shipwrecked Boy. Containi an Account of his Shipwreck, and his Residence alone upon an Uni habited Island. By Mrs. HOFLAN 18mo. Engravings.

THE CLERGYMAN'S O PHAN, and other Tales By Clergyman. For the Use of Yout 18mo. Engravings.

THE ORNAMENTS DISCO ERED. By Mrs. HUGHS. Engr ings.

DIARY OF A PHYSICIA New Edition. 3 vols. 18mo.

NO FICTION: a Narrati founded on Recent and Interesti Facts. By the Rev. ANDRE REED, D.D. New Edition. 12m

MARTHA: a Memorial of only and beloved Sister. By t Rev. ANDREW REED, Author "No Fiction." 12mo.

THE MECHANIC. By Rev. B. TAYLER. 18mo.

LETTERS TO ADA. By t Rev. Dr. PISK. 18mo.

LETTERS OF J. DOWNIN Major, Downingville Militia, Seco Brigade, to his Old Friend M Dwight, of the New-York Daily A vertiser. 18mo. Engravings.

SCENES IN OUR PARIS By a "Country Parson's" Daughte 12mo.

THE SIBYL'S LEAVES. E Mrs. COLEY.

THE NOTE-BOOK OF COUNTRY CLERGYMA 18mo.

FAMILY LIBRARY.

Abundantly illustrated by Maps, Portraits, and other Engravings on steel, copper, and wood.

Nos. 1, 2, 3. The History of the Jews. By the Rev. H. H. Milman.

4, 5. The Life of Napoleon Bona-parte. By J. G. Lockhart, Esq.

6. The Life of Nelson. By Rob-ert Southey, LL.D.

7. The Life and Actions of Alex-ander the Great. By the Rev. J. Williams.

8, 74. The Natural History of I sects.

9. The Life of Lord Byron. B John Galt, Esq.

10. The Life of Mohammed. B the Rev. George Bush.

11. Letters on Demonology an Witchcraft. By Sir Walter Scot Bart.

12, 13. History of the Bible. By the Rev. G. R. Gleig.

14. Narrative of Discovery and Adventure in the Polar Seas and Regions. By Professors Leslie and Jameson, and Hugh Murray.

15. The Life and Times of George the Fourth. By the Rev. George Croly.

16. Narrative of Discovery and Adventure in Africa. By Professor Jameson, and James Wilson and Hugh Murray, Esqrs.

17, 18, 19, 66, 67. Lives of the most Eminent Painters and Sculptors. By Allan Cunningham, Esq.

20. History of Chivalry and the Crusades. By G. P. R. James.

21, 22. The Life of Mary, Queen of Scots. By Henry Glassford Bell, Esq.

23. A View of Ancient and Modern Egypt. By the Rev. M. Russell, LL.D.

24. History of Poland. By James Fletcher, Esq.

25. Festivals, Games, and Amusements. By Horatio Smith, Esq.

26. Life of Sir Isaac Newton. By Sir David Brewster, K.B., &c.

27. Palestine, or the Holy Land. By the Rev. M. Russell, LL.D.

28. Memoirs of the Empress Josephine. By John S. Memes, LL.D.

29. The Court and Camp of Bonaparte.

30. Lives and Voyages of Drake, Cavendish, and Dampier.

31. Description of Pitcairn's Island and its Inhabitants; with an Account of the Mutiny of the Ship Bounty, &c. By J. Barrow, Esq.

32, 72, 84. Sacred History of the World, as displayed in the Creation and Subsequent Events to the Deluge. By Sharon Turner, F.S.A.

33, 34. Memoirs of Celebrated Female Sovereigns. By Mrs. Jameson.

35, 36. Journal of an Expedition to explore the Course and Termination of the Niger. By Richard and John Lander.

37. Inquiries concerning the Intellectual Powers, and the Investigation of Truth. By John Abercrombie.

38, 39, 40. Lives of Celebrated Travellers. By James Augustus St. John.

41, 42. Life of Frederic the Second, King of Prussia. By Lord Dover.

43, 44. Sketches from Venet[ian] History. By the Rev. E. Smedl[ey], M.A.

45, 46. Indian Biography; or, Historical Account of those Indiv[id]uals who have been distinguis[hed] among the North American Nati[ons] as Orators, Warriors, Statesmen, [and] other Remarkable Characters. [By] B. B. Thatcher, Esq.

47, 48, 49. Historical and Desc[rip]tive Account of British India. [By] Hugh Murray, Esq., James Wils[on], Esq., R. K. Greville, LL.D., Whi[te]law Ainslie, M.D., William Rhi[nd], Esq., Professor Jameson, Profes[sor] Wallace, and Captain Clarence D[al]rimple.

50. Letters on Natural Mag[ic] By Dr. Brewster.

51, 52. History of Ireland. By [Thomas] C. Taylor, Esq.

53. Historical View of the Pr[og]ress of Discovery on the North[ern] Coasts of North America. By [P.] F. Tytler, Esq.

54. The Travels and Researc[hes] of Alexander Von Humboldt. [By] W. Macgillivray, A.M.

55, 56. Letters of Euler on Diff[er]ent Subjects of Natural Philosop[hy] Translated by Hunter. With Not[es], &c., by Sir David Brewster and Jo[hn] Griscom, LL.D.

57. A Popular Guide to the [Ob]servation of Nature. By Rob[ert] Mudie.

58. The Philosophy of the Mo[ral] Feelings. By John Abercrombie.

59. On the Improvement of So[ci]ety by the Diffusion of Knowled[ge] By Thomas Dick, LL.D.

60. History of Charlemagne. [By] G. P. R. James, Esq.

61. Nubia and Abyssinia. By t[he] Rev. M. Russell, LL.D.

62, 63. The Life of Oliver Cro[m]well. By the Rev. M. Russell.

64. Lectures on General Lite[ra]ture, Poetry, &c. By James Mo[nt]gomery.

65. Memoir of the Life of Pe[ter] the Great. By John Barrow, Esq[.]

66, 67. The Lives of the m[ost] Eminent Painters and Sculpto[rs] By Allan Cunningham. 2d Serie[s]

68, 69. The History of Arab[ia] By Andrew Crichton.

70. Historical and Descriptive A[c]count of Persia. By James B. F[ra]ser, Esq.

71. The Principles of Physiology applied to the Preservation of Health, and to the Improvement of Physical and Mental Education. By Andrew Combe, M.D.

72. Sacred History of the World. By Sharon Turner, F.S.A. 2d vol.

73. History and Present Condition of the Barbary States. By the Rev. M. Russell, LL.D.

74. The Natural History of Insects. Vol. 2.

75, 76. A Life of Washington. By J. K. Paulding, Esq.

77. The Philosophy of Living. By Caleb Ticknor, A M.

78. The Earth : its Physical Condition and most Remarkable Phenomena. By W. M. Higgins.

79. A Compendious History of Italy. Translated by Nath. Greene.

80, 81. The Chinese. By John Francis Davis, F.R.S.

82. An Historical Account of the Circumnavigation of the Globe, &c.

83. Celestial Scenery; or, the Wonders of the Planetary System displayed. By Thomas Dick, LL.D.

84. Sacred History of the World. By Sharon Turner, F.S.A. Vol. 3.

85. Animal Mechanism and Physiology. By John H. Griscom, M.D.

86, 87, 88, 89, 90, 91. Universal History. By the Hon. Alexander Fraser Tytler and Rev. E. Nares.

92, 93. The Life and Works of Dr. Franklin.

94, 95. The Pursuit of Knowledge under Difficulties ; its Pleasures and Rewards.

96, 97. Paley's Natural Theology. With Notes, &c., by Henry Lord Brougham, Sir Charles Bell, and A. Potter, D.D.

98. Natural History of Birds ; their Architecture, Habits, &c.

99. The Sidereal Heavens, and other Subjects connected with Astronomy. By Thomas Dick, LL.D.

100. Outlines of Imperfect and Disordered Mental Action. By Professor Upham.

CLASSICAL LIBRARY.

With Portraits on steel.

1, 2. Xenophon. (Anabasis, translated by Edward Spelman, Esq., Cyropædia, by the Hon. M. A. Cooper.)

3, 4. The Orations of Demosthenes. Translated by Thomas Leland, D.D.

5. Sallust. Translated by William Rose, M.A.

6, 7. Cæsar. Translated by William Duncan.

8, 9, 10. Cicero. The Orations translated by Duncan, the Offices by Cockman, and the Cato and Lælius by Melmoth.

11, 12. Virgil. The Eclogues translated by Wrangham, the Georgics by Sotheby, and the Æneid by Dryden.

13. Æschylus. Translated by the Rev. R. Potter, M.A.

14. Sophocles. Translated by Thomas Francklin, D.D.

15, 16, 17. Euripides. Translated by the Rev. R. Potter, M.A.

18, 19. Horace. Translated by Philip Francis, D.D. With an Appendix, containing Translations of various Odes, &c., by Ben Jonson, Cowley, Milton, Dryden, &c. And Phædrus. With the Appendix of Gudius. Translated by Christopher Smart, A.M.

20, 21. Ovid. Translated by Dryden, Pope, Congreve, Addison, and others.

22, 23. Thucydides. Translated by William Smith, A.M.

24, 25, 26, 27, 28. Livy. Translated by George Baker, A.M.

29, 30, 31. Herodotus. Translated by the Rev. William Beloe.

32, 33, 34. Homer. Translated by Alexander Pope, Esq.

35. Juvenal. Translated by Charles Badham, M.D., F.R.S. And Persius. Translated by the Rt. Hon. Sir W. Drummond.

36. Pindar. Translated by the Rev. C. A. Wheelwright. And Anacreon. Translated by Thomas Bourne, Esq.

BOYS' AND GIRLS' LIBRARY.

Illustrated by numerous Engravings.

No. 1. Lives of the Apostles and Early Martyrs of the Church.

2, 3. The Swiss Family Robinson; or, Adventures of a Father and Mother and Four Sons on a Desert Island.

4, 13, 18. Sunday Evenings. By the Author of "the Infant Christian's First Catechism."

5. The Son of a Genius. By Mrs. Hofland.

6. Natural History. By Uncle Philip.

7, 8. Indian Traits. By B. B. Thatcher, Esq.

9, 10, 11. Tales from American History. By the Author of "American Popular Lessons."

12. The Young Crusoe; or, the Shipwrecked Boy. By Mrs. Hofland.

14. Perils of the Sea; being Authentic Narratives of Remarkable and Affecting Disasters upon the Deep.

15. Sketches of the Lives of Distinguished Females. By an American Lady.

16. Caroline Westerley; or, the Young Traveller from Ohio. Mrs Phelps (formerly Mrs Lincoln)

17. The Clergyman's Orphan, and other Tales. By a Clergyman.

19. The Ornaments Discovered By Mrs. Hughs.

20. Evidences of Christianity. Uncle Philip.

21. History of Virginia. By Uncle Philip.

22. The American Forest. Uncle Philip.

23, 24. History of New-York. Uncle Philip.

25. Tales of the American Revolution. By B. B. Thatcher.

26, 27. The Whale-fishery and the Polar Seas. By Uncle Philip.

28, 29. History of Massachusetts By Uncle Philip.

30, 31. History of New-Hampshire By Uncle Philip.

SCHOOL DISTRICT LIBRARY.

Illustrated by numerous Engravings.

FIRST SERIES.

Nos. 1, 2. A Life of Washington. By J. K. Paulding, Esq.

3. The Poor Rich Man and the Rich Poor Man. By Miss C. M. Sedgwick.

4, 5. The Swiss Family Robinson; or, Adventures of a Father and Mother and Four Sons on a Desert Island.

6, 7. The Natural History of Insects.

8. The Son of a Genius. By Mrs. Hofland.

9, 10, 11. American History. By the Author of "American Popular Lessons"

12. American Revolution. By B. B. Thatcher, Esq.

13, 14. The Life of Napoleon Bonaparte. By J. G. Lockhart, Esq.

15. The Principles of Physiology applied to the Preservation of Health, and to the Improvement of Physical and Mental Education. By Andrew Combe, M.D.

16, 17. Indian Traits. By B. B. Thatcher, Esq.

18. Narrative of Discovery and Adventure in Africa. By Professor Jameson, and James Wilson and Hugh Murray, Esqrs.

19. The American Forest. Uncle Philip.

20. A Popular Guide to the Observation of Nature. By Robert Mudie

21. Perils of the Sea; being authentic Narratives of Remarkable and Affecting Disasters upon the Deep.

22. Inquiries concerning the Intellectual Powers and the Investigation of Truth. By John Abercrombie, M.D., F.R.S.

23. Lectures on General Literature, Poetry, &c. By James Montgomery.

23

24. Celestial Scenery; or, the Wonders of the Planetary System displayed. By Thomas Dick, LL.D.

25. Palestine; or, the Holy Land. By Rev M. Russell, LL.D.

26. History of Chivalry and the Crusades. By G. P. R. James, Esq.

27. The Life of Sir Isaac Newton. By David Brewster, LL.D.

28. Live and Let Live. By Miss C. M. Sedgwick.

29, 30. The Chinese. By John Francis Davis, F.R S.

31. An Historical Account of the Circumnavigation of the Globe.

32. The Life and Actions of Alexander the Great. By Rev. J. Williams.

33, 34. Letters of Euler on Different Subjects of Natural Philosophy. With Notes and a Life of Euler, by Sir David Brewster; with additional Notes, by John Griscom, LL.D.

35. Memoir of the Life of Peter the Great. By John Barrow, Esq.

36, 37. The Life of Oliver Cro well By Rev. M. Russell, LL.D

38. On the Improvement of Socie by the Diffusion of Knowledge. Thomas Dick, LL.D.

39. The Earth : its Physical Co dition and most Remarkable Pr nomena. By W. M. Higgins.

40. The Philosophy of the Mo Feelings. By John Abercrombie.

41, 42. Memoirs of Celebrated male Sovereigns. By Mrs. James

43. History of Virginia. By U cle Philip.

44. The Ornaments Discover By Mary Hughs.

45. Natural History; or, To and Trades among Inferior Anima By Uncle Philip.

46. 47. The Whale-fishery and t Polar Seas. By Uncle Philip.

48. Lives and Voyages of Ea Navigators.

49, 50. History of New-York. William Dunlap.

SECOND SERIES.

Nos. 51, 52. Life and Works of Dr. Franklin.

53, 54. The Farmer's Instructer; consisting of Essays, Practical Directions and Hints for the Management of the Farm, Garden, &c. By the Hon. Judge Buel.

55, 56. The Pursuit of Knowledge under Difficulties; its Pleasures and Rewards. Illustrated by Memoirs of Eminent Men.

57. Animal Mechanism and Physiology. By J. H. Griscom, M.D.

58. The Elephant as he exists in a Wild State and as he has been made subservient, in Peace and in War, to the Purposes of Man.

59. Vegetable Substances used for the Food of Man.

60, 61, 62, 63, 64, 65. Universal History. By the Hon. Alexander Fraser Tytler and Rev. E. Nares.

66. Illustrations of Mechanics. By Professors Moseley and Renwick.

67. Narrative of Discovery and Adventure in the Polar Seas and Regions. By Professors Leslie and Jameson, and Hugh Murray, Esq.

68. 69. Paley's Natural Theology. With Notes, &c., by Henry Lord Brougham, Sir Charles Bell, and Alonzo Potter, D.D.

70, 71, 72, 73, 74, 75, 76, 77 78, American Biography. Edited Jared Sparks, Esq.

80. The Travels and Research of Alexander Von Humboldt. W. Macgillivray, A.M.

81. The History of Greece. Dr. Goldsmith. Prepared by t Author of "American Popular Le sons," &c.

82. Natural History of Birds.

83. Familiar Illustrations of N ural Philosophy. By Prof. Renwic

84, 85. Selections from the Spe tator.

86. The Elements of Geology. Charles A. Lee, A.M., M.D.

87. The History of Rome. Dr. Goldsmith. Edited by H. Herbert, Esq.

88. A Treatise on Agriculture. Gen. John Armstrong. With Not by the Hon. Judge Buel.

89. Natural History of Quadrupe

90. Chaptal's Chymistry appli to Agriculture.

91. Lives of the Signers of t Declaration of Independence. N. Dwight, Esq.

92, 93, 94, 95. Plutarch's Liv Translated by John Langhorne, D. and William Langhorne, M.A.

The *Third* Series of the School District Library is now in preparation. Among many other valuable works under contract and consideration are the following:

A History of the United States. By the Hon. S. Hale. 2 vols.

History of British America. By Hugh Murray, F.R.S.E.

History of Scotland. By Sir Walter Scott, Bart. 2 vols.

History of France. By E. E. Crowe, Esq. 3 vols.

The History of England. By T. Keightley. 4 vols.

The Science of Mechanics applied to Practical Purposes. By James Renwick, LL.D.

History of the Expedition to Russia undertaken by the Emperor Napoleon. By Gen. Count Philip de Segur. 2 vols.

History of the Fine Arts. By B. J. Lossing, Esq.

Selections from the Works of Dr. Johnson. 2 vols.

Selections from the Works of Dr. Goldsmith.

Selections from the American Poets. By W. C. Bryant, Esq.

Selections from Foreign Poets. By Fitz-Greene Halleck. 2 vols.

The Pleasures and Advantages of Science. By A. Potter, D.D.

Exemplary and Instructive Biography. A new Selection. 3 vols.

The Household Book. By the Rev. Dr. Potter.

Tales from History. By Agnes Strickland. 2 vols.

First Principles of Chemistry familiarly explained. By Professor Renwick.

The Life and Correspondence of Dewitt Clinton. By Professor Renwick.

The Life and Correspondence of General Alexander Hamilton. By Professor Renwick.

The Life and Correspondence of Governor John Jay. By Professor Renwick.

The Life and Travels of Mungo Park.

Parry's Voyages and Journey towards the North Pole. 2 vols.

Life of Patrick Henry. By William Wirt.

Political Economy. Its objects stated and explained, and its Principles familiarly and practically illustrated.

Evening Readings in Nature and Man. Selected and arranged by Alonzo Potter, D.D.

Outlines of Imperfect and Disordered Mental Action. By Professor Upham.

The Starry Heavens and other Objects connected with Astronomy. By Thomas Dick, LL.D.

A familiar Treatise on the Constitution of the United States.

Biographies of Distinguished Females. 2 vols.

Sketches of American Enterprise. 2 vols.

Selections from the Writings of Washington. 2 vols.

The Useful Arts, popularly treated.

The Wonders of Nature and Art.

History of Massachusetts. By Uncle Philip. 2 vols.

History of New-Hampshire. By Uncle Philip. 2 vols.

History of Connecticut. By Theodore Dwight, Esq.

A Valuable and Useful Work for Farmers and Gardeners. By the Editors of " The Cultivator."

A Life of Commodore Perry. By Lieut. A. Slidell Mackenzie.

☞ The first and second series of the School District Library have been pronounced highly judicious, and have been recommended by the public press, the governor of the state, the superintendent of public schools, and other distinguished gentlemen, as the best selection of books that has ever appeared, and, on account of its cheapness and great value, " admirably adapted to the purpose for which it is designed."

The publishers are preparing a fourth series, to consist of books selected by competent persons, and approved by the SUPERINTENDENT OF COMMON SCHOOLS.

The volumes embraced in the School, as well as in the Family, Classical, and Boys' and Girls' Libraries, are sold either separately or in complete sets.

NOVELS, ROMANCES, &c.

MISS EDGEWORTH'S WORKS. 12mo.

Vol. I. Castle Rackrent.—Essay on Irish Bulls.—Essay on Self-Justification.—The Prussian Vase.—The Good Aunt.

Vol. II. Angelina.—The Good French Governess.—Mademoiselle Panache.—The Knapsack.—Lame Jervas.—The Will.—Out of Debt out of Danger.—The Limerick Gloves.—The Lottery.—Rosanna.

Vol. III. Murad the Unlucky—The Manufacturers.—Ennui.—The Contrast.—The Grateful Negro.—To-morrow.—The Dun.

Vol. IV. Manœuvring.—Almeria.—Vivian.

Vol. V. The Absentee.—Madame de Fleury.—Emily de Coulanges. The Modern Griselda.

Vol. VI. Belinda.

Vol. VII. Leonora.—Letters o Female Education—Patronage.

Vol. VIII. Patronage.—Drama

Vol. IX. Harrington.—Though on Bores.—Ormond.

Vol. X. Helen.

⁎ The above can be had sepa ately or in sets.

Practical Education. 12mo.
Frank. 12mo.
Rosamond; and other Storie 12mo.
Harry and Lucy. 2 vols. 12mo.
The Parent's Assistant. 12mo.

MRS. SHERWOOD'S WORKS. 15 vols. 12mo.

Vol. I. Henry Milner, parts I., II., III.

Vol. II. Fairchild Family.—Orphans of Normandy.—The Latter Days.

Vol. III. Little Henry and his Bearer.—Little Lucy and her Dhaye.—Memoirs of Sergeant Dale, his Daughter, and the Orphan Mary—Susan Gray.—Lucy Clare.—Hedge of Thorns—The Recaptured Negro.—Susannah; or, the Three Guardians.—Theophilus and Sophia.—Abdallah, the Merchant of Bagdad.

Vol. IV. The Indian Pilgrim—The Broken Hyacinth.—The Little Woodman—The Babes in the Wood.—Clara Stephens.—The Golden Clew.—Katharine Seward.—Mary Anne—The Iron Cage.—The Little Beggars.

Vol. V. The Infant's Progress.—The Flowers of the Forest—Juliana Oakley—Ermina.—Emancipation.

Vol. VI. The Governess.—The Little Momiere.—The Stranger at Home.—Père la Chaise—English Mary.—My Uncle Timothy.

Vol. VII. The Nun.—Intimate Friends—My Aunt Kate.—Emmeline—Obedience.—The Gipsy Babes.—The Basket-maker.—The Butterfly.—Alune.—Procrastination—The Mourning Queen.

Vol. VIII. Victoria.—Arzoomund.—The Birthday Present.—The Er- rand Boy.—The Orphan Boy—Th Two Sisters.—Julian Percival.—Ed ward Mansfield.—The Infirmary. Mrs. Catharine Crawley—Joan; o Trustworthy.—The Young Foreste —The Bitter Sweet.—Common E rors

Vols IX., X., XI., and XII. Th Lady of the Manor.

Vol. XIII. The Mail-coach.—M Three Uncles—The Old Lady' Complaint—The Hours of Infancy —The Shepherd's Fountain.—Econ omy.—"Hoc Age."—Old Thing and New Things.—The Swiss Cot tage—Obstinacy Punished.—Th Infant's Grave.—The Father's Eye —The Red Book.—Dudley Castle —The Happy Grandmother.—Th Blessed Family.—My Godmother. The Useful Little Girl.—Carolin Mordaunt.—Le Fevre—The Penn Tract.—The Potters' Common The China Manufactory.—Emil and her Brothers.

Vol. XIV. The Monk of Cimiés —The Rosary; or, Rosèe of Mon treux.—The Roman Baths.—Sain Hospice.—The Violet Leaf.—Th Convent of St. Clair.

Vol. XV. The History of Henr Milner, Part IV.—Sabbaths on th Continent.—The Idler.

⁎ The above can be had in set or in separate volumes.

Roxobel. 3 vols. 18mo.

From the Rev. Dr. MILLEDOLER, President of Rutger's College, at New-Brunswick, N. J.

.... *Notwithstanding the objections of some eminent men to the study of the Greek and Roman Classics, it is now almost generally conceded that they form an important if not necessary part of a liberal education.*

A respectable acquaintance with those languages, in which the greatest masters in belles lettres and science have written, cannot be dispensed with by professional men. We do not indeed see, without resorting to these ancient and admired fountains of taste and learning, how elegant literature can be cultivated to advantage, or how even a competent knowledge of our own tongue can be acquired. Whoever, therefore, has so mastered these works that he can teach their grammatical structure not only, but by accurate reference to ancient history, geography, and philology, can trace their nice and varied shades of meaning, unfold their beauty, and inspire the youthful mind with literary enthusiasm, deserves well of the Republic of Letters.

Professor Anthon, in his recent editions of the Classics, has, in the judgment of the undersigned, very ably accomplished this difficult service.

With these works in their hands, our youth will not be left to waste time and mental energy in unnecessary and discouraging investigations, but will be lighted on their way, and excited to exertion.

The typographical part is correctly and elegantly executed.

With my best wishes that both editor and publishers may be amply remunerated by the rapid sale of these works, and their extensive diffusion through the academies and colleges of our country,

I remain, gentlemen,
Yours very respectfully,
PHILIP MILLEDOLER.

From the Rev. JAMES CARNAHAN, D.D., President of the College of New-Jersey, at Princeton, N. J.

Having examined in a cursory manner your series of Anthon's Classical authors, I add, with pleasure, the testimony of my approbation to the numerous recommendations given by others. Professor Anthon's character as a Classical scholar is a sufficient pledge for the accuracy of the edition. If the ability of the learned editor and the neat and handsome appearance of the volumes be justly appreciated, your work cannot fail to receive a liberal patronage.

Your obedient servant,
JAMES CARNAHAN.

From the Rev. Dr. BALDWIN, President of Wabash College, at Crawfordsville, Indiana.

.... *I have read Anthon's Sallust and his Cæsar's Commentaries with much satisfaction. We have adopted the former in the preparatory course connected with our college; and propose to use his editions of Cæsar and of Tully's Orations, in preference to all others. My opinion of the merits of Professor Anthon, as a Latin scholar and editor of the Latin Classics, and particularly as a critical commentator, is very high. I most cheerfully commend his literary labours to the patronage of classical teachers as second to none in his department, with which I am acquainted.*

Yours sincerely,
ELIHU W. BALDWIN.

From the University of St. Louis, Missouri.

..... *We have examined them partly ourselves, and submitted them for farther examination to persons fully competent to pronounce on their merit. We feel happy in stating, that there has been but one opinion on the subject, viz., that the highest encomiums are due to Professor Anthon as a scholar and a friend to education, and that the typographical execution is not inferior to that of the best schoolbooks published in England and in France.....*

Your obedient servants,
J. A. ELET,
Rector of St. Louis University.
J. B. ESNING,
Profes. Ling.

From the Rev. RICHARD H WALL, D.D., Principal of the Preparatory School of Trinity College, Dublin, and Minister of the Chapel Royal.

..... *Doctor Anthon is an admirable commentator. His works have a great sale here. And I shall be anxious to see anything in the Classical way which comes from his pen. We have his Cicero, Sallust, and Horace in general circulation in our schools......*

From the Rev. E. Nott, D.D., President of Union College at Schenectady, N. Y.

The furnishing of our schools and colleges with accurate and uniform editions of the Classical authors in use, accompanied by a useful body of commentary, maps, illlustrations, &c., is an undertaking worthy alike of commendation and of patronage. The competency of Professor Anthon for the editorial supervision assigned him, is well known to me. The whole design meets my entire approbation, and you are quite at liberty to make use of my name in the furtherance of its execution.

Very respectfully,
ELIPHALET NOTT.

From the Rev. F. Wayland, D.D., President of Brown University at Providence, R. I.

I have not been able, owing to the pressure of my engagements, to examine the above works with any degree of accuracy. I however beg leave to thank you for the volumes, and cheerfully bear testimony to the distinguished scholarship of their editor. No classical scholar of our country enjoys a higher reputation, and I know of no one in whose labours more decided confidence may be reposed.

Yours truly,
F. WAYLAND.

From the Rev. John P. Durbin, A.M., President of Dickinson College at Carlisle, Penn.

For some months past my attention has been directed to the series of Classical works now in the course of publication from your press, edited by Professor Anthon. I can with confidence recommend them as the best editions of the several works which have appeared in our country, perhaps in any country. The matter is select, and the notes are copious and clear......

Respectfully,
J. P. DURBIN.

From Thomas R. Ingalls, Esq., President of Jefferson College at St. James, Louisiana.

.....I have examined them with attention, and have no hesitation in saying that I prefer them to any books I have seen for the schools for which they are in- tended. *The editions by Dr. Anth* *seem to me to supply, in a very judici manner, what is wanting to the studen and cannot fail, I should think, to aid restoring Classical studies from the unhappily languishing condition.*

Your obedient servant,
THO. R. INGALLS.

From C. L. Dubuisson, A.M., President of Jefferson College at Washington, Miss.

I have examined with some care t first five volumes of Anthon's Series Classical Works. They are such as should expect from the distinguished e itor. The "Horace" and "Sallus of this gentleman have long been known to me as the very best books to be plac in the hands of a student. As a c mentator, Professor Anthon has, in estimation, no equal. His works ha excited a great and beneficial influen in the cause of Classical learning, a the present undertaking will infinit extend the sphere of that influence. one so well as a teacher can appreci the value of uniform editions of the te. books to be used by his classes. T undertaking of publishing a compl series of all those standard works whi students must read is a noble one, a I sincerely hope it will be complet With such a series as the present pro ises to be, there will be nothing left desire. It is be hoped that editor a publishers will meet with such encoura ment as their truly valuable undertaki deserves.

Your obedient servant,
C. L. DUBUISSON.

From the Rev. John Ludlow, Pre dent of the University of Pennsylvania at Philadelphia.

..... The object is worthy your terprising spirit, and you have been si gularly fortunate in securing the servic of Professor Anthon to direct it to completion. The volumes which y have kindly sent me fully sustain t reputation of that distinguished schol and afford a sure pledge of what may expected in those which are to follo Most heartily do I recommend your u dertaking, and sincerely hope it will m with the encouragement which it rich deserves.

With great respect, yours, &c.,
JOHN LUDLOW.

CPSIA information can be obtained
at www.ICGtesting.com
Printed in the USA
BVHW04*1102170918
527708BV00014B/1516/P